DAVID FLUSFEDER is the author of five previous novels, *Man Kills Woman, Like Plastic*, which won the Encore Award for best second novel, *Morocco, The Gift* and *The Pagan House*. He lives in South London with his family.

From the reviews of *A Film by Spencer Ludwig*:

'A tale of familial bonding involving encounters with the law, prostitutes, poker tables and unsavoury types, all spooled through Spencer's filmic narrative . . . The most memorable sections have the intimacy of a home movie' *Sunday Times*

'Such a joy to read. Spencer's own justification of his life as a "real artist", and his reasons for despising mainstream cinema, are perfectly drawn'   DEBORAH ORR, *Guardian*

'David Flusfeder is a stylishly masculine writer, and he pays fine tribute to the tenacious love that somehow binds this unlikeliest of father-son teams'

HEPHZIBAH ANDERSON, *Daily Mail*

'An exploration of the novel as road movie, complete with gambling, drinking and the Mob. Has the resonance of a film script, with each scene framed for its visual potential. Flusfeder is inventive and treads the fine line between comedy and tragedy with considerable wit and skill'

Mail on Sunday

By the same author

The Pagan House
The Gift
Morocco
Like Plastic
Man Kills Woman

DAVID FLUSFEDER

A Film by Spencer Ludwig

FOURTH ESTATE · London

Fourth Estate
An imprint of HarperCollins*Publishers*
77–85 Fulham Palace Road
Hammersmith
London W6 8JB

Visit our authors' blog at www.fifthestate.co.uk
Love this book? www.bookarmy.com

This Fourth Estate paperback edition published 2011
1

First published in Great Britain by Fourth Estate in 2010

A catalogue record for this book is available from the British Library

ISBN 978-0-00-725032-5

Printed and bound in Great Britain by Clays Ltd, St Ives plc

Mixed Sources
Product group from well-managed
forests and other controlled sources
www.fsc.org   Cert no. SW-COC-001806
© 1996 Forest Stewardship Council

For Grace

Chapter One

Spencer Ludwig, film-maker, arrives at his father's apartment somewhat out of sorts.

He dawdles at the threshold. Blue carpet, brown walls, black door, he looks for something that will strengthen him against the inevitable onslaught of his father's and step-mother's world. If he had a camera with him, he would use it—extreme close-up: the carpet, his sneakers, the apartment door. Before pressing the bell he would whisper, and he does, *Here goes.*

Spencer has become a frequent visitor to his father's apart-ment. He has made this journey—tube from Stockwell to Heathrow, plane to JFK, subway to 50th Street—four times already this year, arriving, like this, encumbered by luggage and laptop, sticky and half dazed. His father, the idol and enemy of Spencer's youth, is eighty-six years old and in failing health.

'Here goes,' he repeats.

Voices are raised from inside the apartment, as they often are. *Jimmy?!* his stepmother yells, unanswered, maybe unanswerable.

TALK TO ME! Spencer has dawdled long enough, but he lingers some more. Coming out of the subway station, sweating under the weight of his luggage on a cold spring day, he had walked past his father's apartment building and the Museum of Modern Art and steeled himself with a double espresso and a half-hour of internet poker at a coffee shop on 6th Avenue. There he had sat squeezed at the window between an almost respectably dressed young man and a blonde woman of unearthly thinness. The young man occupied himself in expectorating and muttering. The woman pecked away at her laptop. Spencer tried to keep his attention upon his own laptop and avoid contact with the young man's sounds or the bird woman's words on her screen.

HUNTER
I guess that's pretty lame.

Hunter, he presumed, was a male character, based, as cruelly as her thin vengeful yearning could make him, on her most recent disappointing boyfriend.

Spencer played poker. He clicked and bet and clicked and bet and folded and clicked and raised and reraised and clicked. He was late to see his father, and he wasn't winning in this session, and its instrumental purpose became lost in the seedy relentlessness of the pursuit itself. Spencer, so tentative in most areas of his life, is ferocious in pursuit and defence of his work, ferocious in his love for his daughter, Mary, and ferocious, sometimes obsessional, in his playing of poker. Once, in Paris in autumn, during a film festival, he stayed all night in his hotel room, eschewing screenings and dinners and parties and meetings with distributors in favour of screen-staring, of clicking and betting and clicking.

A lucky river when he was foolishly chasing a draw against a competent opponent who was extracting the maximum from his top two pairs won Spencer $225. Before he lost the little he had left in his online account, and became too offended by the swirling clutches of mucus and saliva from the young gentleman on his right and the dismal work of the woman on his left

HUNTER

I know. I'm sorry. But I do love
you, you know. That cute thing
you do with your mouth, I just
want to kiss it.

he put his laptop in its case and hoisted his load and went to his father's apartment.

Here goes. And it is all going full throttle in there, geriatric rage, the hatefulness of old people who have terminally disappointed each other. Spencer's father is sitting at the table in the corner of the living room working on a jigsaw puzzle, dwarfed by the skyscrapers through the high glass windows that arouse a giddy vertigo in Spencer. His wife is stumping and ranting around the apartment, and Spencer's stepbrother, Jacksie, is walking after his mother, trying to appease while giving her further fuel to go on.

Jacksie is in his late fifties, but apart from some issues with his prostate and a spreading of the gut, he wouldn't seem much more than forty or so. He dresses as he has always done, as a sporty suburban child, in shorts and sweatshirt, and the only alarming things about his appearance are the perpetual hurt look in his eyes and the blizzardy whiteness of his teeth. Jacksie lives in California, which is where his teeth are from.

'I want a toaster-oven,' Spencer's stepmother says, spitting out the words as if the world is denying her a basic human right, which she will avenge even if governments should fall and stars be extinguished.

'You'll get your toaster-oven,' Jacksie says.

'Well where is it?!' his mother says.

'Hey Spencer, what's up?' Jacksie says.

'Hello Jacksie.'

'Look Pop! Look who's here! You know who this is?'

Jacksie treats Spencer's father as if he is an imbecile, which Jimmy Ludwig can hardly ever be bothered any more to resent.

Spencer's father has a very nice smile. Sometimes it is even sincere, as it seems to be now, as he gets up from the table and walks over, stooped and frail, to greet his son. Spencer pulls away the trailing oxygen tube that has become wrapped around his left ankle, and they hug. Before Spencer receives his inevitable insult from his father about his appearance, he reflects that an ease that was entirely absent from their relationship is now present. They used to make each other physically uncomfortable. Spencer tries to remember when he stopped fearing his father.

Jimmy Ludwig used to be an attorney, specialising in corporate law, patents disputes, the breaking of international contracts. He came over to the US with his English wife after having spent an uncomfortable few years as a Polish immigrant in London after the War. He worked as an engineer in a factory while attending law classes at City College. Sometimes he joked that his first wife was cheaper than language classes.

After he became successful he developed a taste for Italian suits, the dapper effect spoiled only a little by the trousers always being cinched and belted to one side, his propensity to collect food stains on his shirt and tie. He carried on working until seven years ago, when he suffered a stroke that deprived him of some of his powers of expression and comprehension. In the past year, his body has started to disintegrate. Now he sits in a room and is rude to his wife and solves jigsaw puzzles and watches boxing on TV in between visits to doctors who give him sampler packs of speculative medications and tell him they can do nothing for him.

Neither he nor his second wife is capable of looking after themselves or each other. Despite Spencer's history with his father, he has found himself, for motivations he doesn't quite understand, being a dutiful and attentive son.

When Spencer is in New York, he ferries his father to doctors' appointments and plays backgammon against him, remorseless competition for twenty-five cents a point, with breaks for meals, when Spencer's father either quarrels with Spencer's stepmother or eats in a morose efficient silence, while Spencer makes occasional attempts to heal his father's marriage, and he is always relieved when the week is over.

'Still best-dressed man,' Spencer's father says.

Spencer dresses badly out of a sort of principled vanity. Believing that a gentleman should either be a dandy or a schlump, he wears a uniform of black sneakers and baggy black jeans and loose fitting black T-shirts with a faded image or logo on them.

'How are you doing?' Spencer says.

'I'm doing shit,' Spencer's father says. 'Good to see you.'

'And you.'

Spencer's stepmother takes a moment to greet Spencer. He wonders, ever since he was a child he has wondered, why she always manages to leave lipstick smears on her front top teeth. He would have thought that she would have noticed this by now or that her husband would have pointed it out, but Spencer's father no longer talks to his wife.

'I fell over. Do you want to see the bruise?' she says to Spencer.

Spencer, without meaning to, takes a step back in recoil.

'Uh. No. It's OK,' he says.

'There are some things a stepson shouldn't see!' Jacksie yells.

His voice is always full-volume, as if he is accustomed to dealing with the nearly deaf.

'We're going to Gribitz,' Spencer's father says.

Spencer's father has problems with his lungs, his blood

pressure, the nerve endings of his hands and feet, he is in constant pain from stenosis of the spine; but he is most concerned about his inability to empty his bowels.

'Pop's got a lot of issues with his BMs,' Jacksie says.

Jacksie always calls Spencer's father *Pop*, even though he had his own father once and, apart from one excursion to Kennedy Airport when Jacksie was young, there has never been any aspect of their relationship that could be described as father–son.

'Charlie,' says Spencer's father.

Charlie is his default name for any man. When Spencer was young, his father would sometimes consent to tell his son bedtime stories set in the War. There were three characters, Steve, Mike and their leader, Charlie. Charlie was the daring one, who would, with ingenuity and audacity, deliver the pals from evil and imminent death. Spencer had initially projected himself as Charlie but then accepted that he was as yet unworthy of the role and decided instead that it was his father's name for himself.

'I've got something to show you that you're going to love,' Jacksie says. 'Sit down. Make yourselves comfortable.'

Spencer angles his father's chair to face the television set and sits beside him. Waiting for their appreciation is a DVD of Jacksie's home in southern California. Jacksie, after some struggles to comprehend the workings of the remote control which Spencer longs to tear out of his hand, manages to solve the problem of how to press the play button.

Jacksie sits on a smaller chair that is closer to the television.

'This is my home,' he says. 'A friend of mine did this. I think you'll find it's very good.'

On the screen, Jacksie and his wife Ellie wave at the camera from a terrace. There are vines in large urns beside them. A verdant hillside behind them is dotted with similar houses, Spanish colonial style, white stucco walls, terracotta roofs.

'On a clear day you can see all the way to Catalina,' Jacksie says.

He sits forward avidly watching as if he were seeing it for the very first time.

'What do you think of the camerawork?' Jacksie asks.

'I think it's execrable,' Spencer says.

'Yeah, it's good isn't it?'

Spencer's father has fallen asleep. Spencer surreptitiously photographs him with the camera on his mobile phone. There are new messages on it, from his daughter, which he wants to respond to, and from his producer, whom he is seeking to avoid.

'Hey! Spence! I hope you're paying attention!'

'Yes. Oh. Sorry.'

Spencer returns his attention to the screen. An urn of grapes, a dying spaniel, a shot of Jacksie and Ellie on their veranda accompanied by a dreary plinkety-plonk of a faux jazz sound-track.

'Jerry, who filmed this, composed the music himself,' Jacksie says.

'Yes, well, I suppose he might have,' Spencer says.

When the thing is finally over, Spencer feels compelled to say something nice.

'Well, your house is very beautiful,' he says.

'It certainly is!' Jacksie says. 'My little piece of Eden. I bet you really want to visit us now.'

'I do. Seeing this makes me want to see it in person.'

'It would have exactly the same effect on me,' Jacksie says.

And back in stumps Jacksie's mother, Spencer's stepmother, Spencer's father's second wife. When Spencer first met her, thirty-five years before, she was a tanned suburban beauty. He was six years old, she affected to adore him. Now her skin is heavily lined, her eyes are bitter and narrow, her limbs and back are bent and crooked, and her scalp can be seen through the sprayed dyed helmet of her hair, which she has tended to once a week at the ironically named beauty parlour. She is seventy-four, twelve years younger than her husband. They have been married for thirty-four years, far longer than either were with their first spouses.

'I think we need a day bed,' she says.

'OK,' Jacksie says.

'We're going to need help here. I can't ask someone to sleep on the sofa. Don't you think so, Spencer?'

'Yes. I suppose so.'

'Jimmy!' she yells, waking up her husband. 'I'm talking about the day bed!'

Jimmy Ludwig slowly opens his eyes. He fixes a look of uttter pained hopelessness on to his wife that comes close to breaking his son's heart, shakes his head, which produces a corresponding wince of pain, and stands up to inspect his jigsaw puzzle with his chin pressed uncomfortably to his chest.

'Where's your collar? Jimmy! I said, Where's your collar?'

He does not risk a movement of the head this time. He lifts a jigsaw piece, which might be an azure tip of one of the flowers in a pot beside four ginger kittens, and inspects it by rolling his eyes up so he can just about see it from the painful angle that his vision is forced to examine the world from.

'Dad,' Spencer says. 'You should probably put on your collar.'

Spencer retrieves his father's neck brace from beneath the magazine rack, where it had fallen, or been discarded, on to a pile of his father's completed jigsaw puzzles.

Spencer's father accepts the collar, a wide strip of yellow foam bandaged by a strip of white cloth that has become a little grubby through frequent use. He wraps it around his damaged neck, a strip of Velcro seals it shut, and his chin is supported, and lifted a little. He makes another little grunt, which might be of protest, or acceptance—although that is unlikely—but the noise is partly lost in the constant low rumble and hiss of his oxygen machine.

Spencer's father's first name was originally Izio. (His last name was originally Lewissohn, but that was discarded a couple of generations before he was born.) When he arrived in London he thought it advisable to have an English-sounding name, as if that would somehow obscure his utter foreignness. He attempted to call himself Tim, because that was the name of a colonel he had served under whose manners had impressed him. Meeting his future first wife at a Polish ex-servicemen's dance in Clapton, he tried out his adopted name. In his thick accent, the word came out sounding more like Jim, which was what she called him. He was too embarrassed, for both of them, to correct her, and so he was, as it were, christened.

'I want to have the day bed over there,' Spencer's stepmother says.

'That's where Pop sits,' Jacksie says.

'Don't you think I need a day bed?'

'I'm not saying you don't. That's not the issue,' Jacksie says.

'Tell me then. What is the *issue*?'

Jacksie seldom stands up to his mother, so his effort now is quite impressive. Nonetheless, he looks to Spencer for support, and lifts his hands, as if to protect his face.

'Don't you think,' Spencer says, 'that you could have the day bed, without disruption? Maybe you could put it over there, against that wall.'

'I don't want it against that wall. I want it here.'

'But. That's where my father sits,' Spencer says. 'That's where his chair is.'

'The chair can move!'

'Maybe,' Jacksie says, emboldened by having an ally, by he and his stepbrother outnumbering, if not outvoicing, his mother, 'maybe Pop doesn't want the chair to move.'

Spencer's stepmother explodes in self-pity and rage.

'You know what I don't like around here?! No one cares

about me. No one asks me how I am! The toaster-oven has been broken for three days!'

'Don't worry, Mom. We'll get you a new toaster-oven,' Jacksie says.

'All we're saying,' Spencer says, 'is that you can have a day bed and my father doesn't have to move his chair. There's enough room here for both.'

His stepmother ignores him, turns her spite on to her son.

'And let me tell you something. You want to hear something? I don't care any more. I don't want a fucking toaster-oven.'

And with that, she stumps off again, before stumping back in again to remind Spencer that his father has an appointment with Dr Gribitz in just under an hour.

'Mom?' Jacksie says.

'Don't fucking Mom me,' Spencer's stepmother says, and stumps back towards the bedroom on her crooked legs. (The soul writes itself on the body.)

'Do you mind if I use the phone?' Spencer says.

'Of course I do!' his father says in an attempt at humour.

'Be quick,' his stepmother says, poking her head around the bedroom door. 'You're taking Dad to Gribitz.'

His first call is to Cheryl Baumbach at the Short Beach Film Festival.

'I'm here in New York,' Spencer says.

'That's great. That's terrific.'

'Coming down tomorrow, I hope. I just wanted to check that you had received my DVDs'.

'I'm sure we have.'

'Particularly *Robert W's Last Walk*. For the retrospective.'

'For the . . .?'

'You said you wanted to screen all my films.'

'Well we do. Of course we do. We're very excited.'

She does not sound excited. She sounds absent, almost

uninterested, and Spencer's stepmother returns to fuss and flurry around them and Spencer's father continues to ignore her.

'Spencer!'

'Yes,' he says to his stepmother. 'Just one more call.'

He signs off to Cheryl Baumbach with an attempt at the sort of benevolent charm one might expect from a director whom festivals deem worthy of a retrospective and then he calls his daughter.

Mary is ten years old. She is air whereas he is earth, free where he is most trammelled. Her company delights and somewhat intimidates him. Her mother, to whom he was nearly married, is sensible, and worldly. The period when he was with her, when he had temporarily learned to clean the dishes the same day they were dirtied, to wash the basin after he shaved, to respond to a direct question with more than a grunt, had lifted Spencer in the opinion of his father, an unearned respect that he has not entirely squandered.

Mary has a cold and she is looking for something from him that will make her feel better. Mary has a direct relationship to the world that usually involves acquisition.

'Daddy. Will you get me an iPod?'

'No honey. I won't get you an iPod.'

'Why not? You're in *America*. You're in *New York*.'

'You're ten years old. You don't need an iPod.'

He does not need to listen to the list of her friends who own iPods, the Roses and Lilys and Poppys and all the others, who stand out, pink skinned, yellow haired, floral named, from the Shinequas and Taaliyahs and Chanels at her primary school (and who, presumably, do not own iPods or iTouches or iTastes). Unspoken but loudly declared in the list she reels off are all the indignities and unfairnesses of her life, and the precariousness of her loyalty to Spencer.

'Spencer! Gribitz!'

'Yes yes. I know. Look, honey. I have to go in a moment. I'm taking Papa Jimmy to his proctologist.'

She does not ask what a proctologist is, because Mary, like her mother, does not wish to appear unknowledgeable about any subject. But showing off his vocabulary of fancy medical terms will not protect him from his daughter's needs or scorn.

His daughter does not have to stay loyal to him. There is another man in her world, whose name is Doug. Mary's mother has demonstrated her preference for Doug over Spencer so why shouldn't Mary feel the same way? She lives with him and Doug has money, so Doug can buy her an i-anything if only she would ask him—it is a tattered piece of loyalty that impels her to persist with Spencer anyway. *And* she has a headache. *And* her stomach hurts. She is off school and Mummy has said that she may not go to Grace's party, which is unfair.

'Not if you're sick, honey,' Spencer says, nobly resisting the opportunity to join forces with his daughter against her mother.

Spencer had tried to be a family man. He had done what he thought was his best at making a go of it, family Christmases, family holidays, but he had not convinced anyone of his sincerity, least of all himself.

Mary's mother made more money than Spencer did and she saw the world rather as Spencer's father did, a straightforward place where value was measurable by money, in which the person who owned the most things was the winner.

'Errol Flynn said that if he left behind any money after he died then his life would have been a failure.'

'Who's Errol Flynn?'

And Spencer's stepmother continues to stamp around. *Gribitz . . . Dad . . . appointment . . . Car!*

'A movie star, baby,' Spencer says.

'I've never heard of him,' says Mary, dismissing Errol Flynn utterly and perhaps with him the entire Hollywood Golden Age.

When Mary was born, Spencer made the mistake of announcing that he had received his emotional pension plan, here was someone who would look after him when he was old and friendless. Sometimes he aroused the maternal instinct in her, often they had fun, usually they could make each other laugh. But at other times she was like a highly strung puppy made peevish and insecure by the ineffectualness of its owner.

'I've got a stomach ache. Will you get me an iPod?'

Generously, she is giving him a final chance, and how he wants to say yes, a part of a father's job is to protect a child's innocence, and why shouldn't he pretend along with her that buying luxury goods is a cure for most conditions?

'Look. I—'

But his stepmother finally intervenes. She can bear this no longer. Her world is manageable only when she is charge of all of its details, and to her this is unbearable, that her nebbish of a stepson is enjoying himself on the telephone when the routine demands he now be making the call to the garage to release the car.

'The doctor! The garage! Dad's appointment! *Gribitz!*'

'I'm sorry,' Spencer says (and how he hates himself for making an apology, even such an unreflective one). 'I'm talking to my daughter. She's sick.'

His stepmother inhales and exhales rather dramatically before speaking. She looks magnificently triumphant.

'Well we're *sicker!*'

'I'm sorry, honey, I'd better go. I'm taking Papa Jimmy to his doctor.'

'I hate you! You're rubbish!'

'Oh,' he says, but he is talking to air.

Jacksie is moving his hands ineffectually into and out of his pockets. Spencer's stepmother is carrying small plastic bags containing a variety of small coloured objects. Spencer's father is struggling into his jacket, refusing any assistance. And how Spencer wants to film this. Obtaining the release might be problematical but people are vain, and usually want to be on screen, regardless of the circumstances.

He hasn't allowed himself any equipment. Usually Spencer carries a small camera with him. Recently, between jobs (Michelle, his sometimes producer, has been calling, but Spencer can't talk to her), he has been gathering autobiographical footage to use in a speculative future film, in which he supposes that images ripped away from context (physical, emotional) will be montaged with stock footage, crowd scenes, moments of intimacy or war. But his most recent girlfriend, Abbie, had grown tired of this. She had been one of his students and he had failed her on the course just to prove that this was not some clichéd master–servant relationship. This had made her angry. *You think it's because you're some kind of artist, and some others even think so too. But I'm not fooled any more. It's because you're frightened of real life, you need to put something between you and real life.*

Expertly, rather cruelly, he had demolished her childish notions of *real life*. But all the same, as he packed to leave for the airport, he deliberately left his camera behind. He would show her that he had no need for filtering or mediating experience. And he would prove it so well that he would have no need to report his triumph back to Abbie.

Spencer has almost given up on his ambition to produce a single great film. If he were to be honest with himself, which sometimes he is, then he would have to admit that he has not entirely given up believing this might be possible, that the films of Ludwig could join the team, Ruttman, Vertov, Fassbinder, Reed, Lang, some Marker, Ray, Dreyer, Ford, Buñuel, Bresson, Hawks, Wilder. The list could go on; but even if his films were doomed never to join the A-list, he would want at least a shot or two to enter the minds of his audience and be installed there, a single glorious image, with all the vividness of lived experience or unforgettable dream.

Man without a movie camera went to New York. Images that have interested him along the way he has recorded with his telephone. He will allow himself this, he decided. Just as long as nothing is altered or arranged for the picture.

His father disentangles himself from his oxygen machine, and crumblingly attaches himself to one of his portable cylinders.

'Let's get out of this shithole,' he says.

There is silence and then some confusion in the room.

'*What* did he say?' Spencer's stepmother says.

Jacksie winks at Spencer's father and then at Spencer.

'Still the dude, Jimmy. You the man! High-five!'

Spencer's father ignores him. He has the portable oxygen cylinder switched on and the breathing tube attached to at least one nostril.

'Toaster-oven,' Spencer says. 'He says we'll get the toaster-oven.'

'Oh. Are you sure? He's already been out once today. Jimmy?! YOU'VE ALREADY BEEN OUT TODAY. YOU MUST BE TIRED!'

Spencer's father ignores her as he always does. He looks lavishly away and continues to fumble with the breathing tube. Spencer's stepmother considers the situation. It does not make her unhappy for her husband to be away from her if he is in the care, and responsibility, of his son.

'You'll need something to eat.'

'We won't need anything to eat,' Spencer says.

'His blood-sugar levels shouldn't get too low. A little and often is what Dr Kornblut says. At least take some fruit. JIMMY? WOULD YOU LIKE A PIECE OF FRUIT? I'VE PACKED YOU A PLUM AND A BANANA IN A BAGGIE.'

'It's the old Jimmy. Decisive, man of action. You see that, Mom?' Jacksie says.

'Here,' says Spencer's father, impotently holding out the dangling breathing tube.

Spencer fixes the tube while his stepmother stumps out of the living room, and then she comes in again and stumps out and back, bringing more items each time, until Spencer has the portable oxygen cylinder in a carry-bag, the spare cylinder in a rucksack along with one baggie that contains a banana and two plums (which Spencer resolves to take a photograph of as soon as they are out into the hallway), another baggie with Spencer's father's medications, a fold-up umbrella, a sweater, four Pepperidge Farm Milano cookies, which she knows that Spencer likes and which prove that she is not entirely without a sense of care and fellow-feeling, and some sections of the *New York Times*.

'Mom. They're only going out to the doctor,' Jacksie says.

'You want to come with us? Maybe it'll be fun,' Spencer asks.

'Sure. But no, I better stay here with Mom.'

'Maybe you should take your two o'clock medicines now.'

Spencer's father spectacularly ignores his wife.

'Don't you think that's a good idea, Spencer? Honey? Spencer thinks it's a good idea.'

Spencer's father averts his head from whichever direction his wife approaches. She reaches to wipe his hair back into place and he bats her hand away.

'Your medicines,' she says, and Spencer's father ignores her.

'Why don't you take your medicine,' Spencer says, and his father makes an all-things-are-meaningless gesture and grumpily holds out his hand for the pills.

He is on sertraline for his depression and prednisone for his breathing and proamatine to raise his blood pressure and rosu-vastatin to lower his cholesterol and tramadol for back pain and fludrocortisone for his adrenal gland and alfuzosin to shrink his prostate and darifenacine to calm his bladder and aspirin to stave off another stroke. Spencer's stepmother keeps all the medications, his and hers, in little white boxes that have separate compartments for the days of the week.

'And the spare oxygen. Don't forget the spare oxygen.'

Spencer says, *I won't*, and checks the gauge reading on the portable oxygen tank.

'Two,' his father says.

'It's on two,' Spencer says. And Spencer checks the volume on the spare oxygen tank and puts it in the tote-bag along with his father's cap and scarf and his stepmother's discarded sections of the *New York Times*.

'Have you called for the car?' Spencer's stepmother says and Spencer says that he has and tells his father, *We're all set*.

'Take the cane,' Spencer's stepmother says, and Spencer nods and finds the cane in its place under the hall table, which has mail ready to be sent secured under the base of a carved wooden Buddha, a souvenir from a trip to South-East Asia made in the days before she got sick.

'Don't forget the toaster-oven,' Spencer's stepmother says.

'Where's the affidavit?' Spencer's father says.

'What's he saying?' Spencer's stepmother says. 'What affidavit?'

And Spencer is familiar enough with his father's mind to know that he is referring to something non-legal that he has decided is integral to their outing. One of the symptoms of his aphasia is that he tends to substitute a word that he was accustomed to use for work for something that he requires in the present.

'What?' says Spencer. 'Your pills? You've taken them.'

His father irritably shakes his head.

'The affidavit,' he says, and shakes his right hand in a loosely held fist.

'What's he saying?' Spencer's stepmother says. 'Why is he

doing that? That tremor is new. Do you think we should take him back to the neurologist?'

By *we* Spencer's stepmother means *you*. She cannot bear to be alone with her husband any more.

'I think I get it. You mean the backgammon?' Spencer says. His father nods, no less irritably.

'That's what I said, the affidavit.'

Spencer adds the backgammon set to the tote-bag and their preparations are complete. His father consents to take the cane in his left hand. Spencer's stepmother stumps along with them for their journey to the elevator, which is precarious because Spencer's father just follows his own erratic path, making no allowances for the tube that connects his nose to the oxygen cylinder that Spencer is carrying. Spencer, with the tote-bag over his right shoulder, the cylinder over his left (and both hands poised to catch his father should he fall), has to twist and skip to keep the oxygen tube straight. The elevator operator is a kind man who has grown old inside his brown uniform. The badge he wears on the breast pocket of his jacket announces just his first name.

'How are you doing today, Mister Ludwig? Mister Ludwig.'

It is only recently that Spencer has been honoured by being greeted formally by the doormen and elevator operators of his father's building. In former times his appearance had been too disreputable, his manner too odd by Museum Tower standards, to merit more than a nod, a request every time he stepped into the elevator for his floor number, even though he had been visiting his father and stepmother here for close to twenty years. But the group mind of the building's staff had promoted Spencer in the aftermath of his father's stroke and his display of dutiful care to the rank of someone to whom it was appropriate to show respect.

Spencer's father stumbles into the elevator, and relievedly allows himself to fall against its rear wall with his hands behind him in case he needs to push off again.

'Thank you James.'

'You're welcome, Mister Ludwig.'

Spencer's father waits in the lobby of his building with his oxygen tank and the supplies for their journey while Spencer walks the half-block to the garage where Spencer's father keeps his car. He holds the dollar bill that his father has given him to tip the car-jockey with and which Spencer obscurely resents.

He has tried to persuade his father to sell the car. It costs money to maintain and garage. He hardly uses it, indeed he shouldn't use it at all because of his medical conditions, and when his son comes to visit him, he is the one to drive it, a black Cadillac El Dorado that had been new six years before, but now is battered and dented from his father's geriatric adventures in city traffic. Despite his attempts to persuade his father to surrender the car, Spencer likes driving it. It is a much better car than the one he has in London.

Chapter Two

When he was young, and visiting his father in New York, his father would be there to meet him at the airport, pacing in the Arrivals lounge in impatience and anticipation and perhaps even pleasure at seeing his son, who would materialise holding a stewardess's hand, blinking in mother-chosen clothes that were creased and hateful to him from seven hours on a transatlantic flight, or, a few years later, slouching through, his late-teenaged self, dressing to be the person he hoped to become, in jeans and a ripped leather jacket—and his father's mood, whether it was born out of nervousness or love, would show itself in a suddenness that felt like aggression. In the car from the airport, questions would be hurled by Jimmy Ludwig at his son, *How's school? How's your social life? How's your mother? What scores did you get on your tests? When are you going to decide what you're going to do with your life? Guess what? Guess what? I'll give you three guesses and the first two don't count*, which were all the more alarming as he seemed to be giving the better part of his attention to the road, twisting his car at high speed within the traffic, yelling, *Move it Charlie!* to anyone who held up his progress.

His father's Americanness had manifested itself early in an aptitude for hard work, a disregard for anyone who didn't have the smarts or the stamina to get on in life, and tastes for chewing gum and television and cars. His father's decline, or, rather, his father's announcement of his consciousness of his decline, had shown itself for the first time a few years ago, on what had been supposedly an ordinary visit of Spencer's into his father's world, when they were setting off for a downtown restaurant and he passed his keys to Spencer and sat down, uncomplaining and humble, in the passenger seat.

Ever since then, Spencer has always been the designated driver of his father's car, an accession to power that is not without constraint or perpetual accountability.

Driving through midtown Manhattan after the appointment with Dr Gribitz, Spencer has been telling his father about the Short Beach Film Festival, because an obscure part of himself that he would like to disown is still hungry for his father's approval.

'Take a right,' his father says, gesturing impatiently at the limousine that is hogging the lane in front of them.

'OK.'

Spencer indicates and shifts into the right lane, though the traffic there is even less mobile, because of the bus a block ahead, which is struggling to manoeuvre past some roadworks.

'Right! I said right!'

And his father angrily lifts away the oxygen tube to wipe some of the spit that has collected on his chin.

'I *am* going right!'

'Right! RIGHT!'

'OK. You win.'

And Spencer twists the wheel with more assurance and speed than he can usually summon up and possess, and blisters the

El Dorado across two lanes to the left, barely missing the front of a taxicab and just shaving the rear bumper of a truck.

'That's more like it,' his father says, sitting back in his seat and looking at his son with an expression that Spencer can't register because he is too nervously looking straight ahead.

Tomorrow will be a fuller day, with appointments at the urologist, the pulmonarist and the optometrist. But already today his father has been poked, prodded, X-rayed, sono-grammed and MRIed. Now they are driving south down Park Avenue, and the day has been horrible and uncomfortable for them both and Spencer does not want it to end like this.

'You hungry?' Spencer asks.

'Not really,' his father says.

'Maybe we should stop there?' he says, pointing over to the Hooters sign. 'Get a burger, a milk shake, and stare at the wait-resses' . . . you know . . .'

He is bashful with his father, always has been. The two of them had never found an adequate way of being with each other. What had begun as physical unease had spread to an emotional discomfort and even, in some sort of way, a moral one.

'What, you know?' his father asks, and Spencer doesn't know if he is being teased or toyed with or just being asked a question that is simple and direct.

'They have, you know . . .'

And he gestures with his cupped right hand, lifting air in front of his chest and winking in a most uncomfortable way.

'Keep your hands on the wheel,' his father says.

'Breasts, big breasts,' he says.

His father laughs. It is nearly soundless apart from the wheezing for air and a little mucus sliding up and down his nose. Spencer wonders if it is he who is being laughed at or the idea of the two of them sitting in a restaurant staffed by young women with big breasts or, just for a moment, the indig-nity of his own condition and age.

Stuck in traffic, Spencer's father has been slumbering. Abruptly, he comes to.

'Oh shit. I forgot to go to the men's room.'

And Jimmy Ludwig in the passenger seat looks shamefully down at the wet patch spreading on his groin.

The turn to 53rd Street is ahead, a bus waits for a herd of tourists to finish crossing the road, and it is all preordained, to drop his father off outside his building, the near-silent comedy (grunts and panting for a soundtrack) of the doorman helping his father and his burdens out of his seat, and the car dropped off at the garage, the return into the apartment where some zones are freezing and others tropical hot, because Jimmy Ludwig and his wife have a very different sensitivity to temperature, and to sit, and wait, and wilt. Anything, especially the unknown, would be better than this. Spencer does not take the turn to 53rd Street.

'What are you doing?' his father says.

'I thought maybe we'd go on an excursion.'

'Terrific,' his father says. 'What a terrific idea.'

If this were an independent film, Spencer considers, they would not be allowed to return to the apartment and sit in the dimness of his father's decline, chilled by the storm of his step-mother's neuroses. He keeps on driving, south along Park Avenue.

'Where are we going?' his father asks.

'I don't know. Maybe we should visit the town where I was born.'

'Why would we want to do that?' his father says, and, closing his eyes, drifts away to a place that is accessible to none but the very sick.

'You always were a cold-hearted bastard,' the son says to the father. His father is sitting in the passenger seat, mouth agape, oxygen fitting trailing out of one nostril, eyes closed, snoring with his laboured breath. Spencer realises, to his shame, that he would not have dared say this unless he knew his father was asleep.

'Fuck you too,' Jimmy Ludwig says, not bothering to open his eyes.

Spencer goes into the right lane on Park Avenue, takes the turn on to 42nd Street. If this were an independent film, the sort that juries on competitions favour (and even Spencer's own difficult slow movements of anguish and observation have been rewarded with prizes), then it would turn into a road movie, father and son driving down an American highway with the sound of the radio and his father's oxygen tank for company.

'Ninety-Six Tears,' says Spencer. 'Mexicali Baby.'

'What are you saying?'

'I was thinking about the soundtrack.'

'What?'

'For this. Us. If this were an independent movie, I'd have 1960s garage punk and maybe some classical. Schubert. Late Beethoven quartets. The Stooges. Rio Rockers. That's what I'd have. Maybe some blues. Blind Willie Johnson. And Dylan. But he probably charges too much. *Basement Tapes.*'

His father stares at him. He shakes his head slowly.

His father used to say to him, *When they made you they threw away the mould.* Which Spencer in his naivety had at first thought of as an announcement of respect, a recognition of his particularness. But then he realised that it was just a customary fatherly rejection of anything or anyone he failed to understand.

'Watch out. She's got her eye on you.'

They have a police car for company. The very male cop is scrutinising them for signs of illegality. Ever since his stroke, Spencer's father has designated most men as *she*. His brain-damaged mistakes with pronouns make him sound like an elderly, cantankerous homosexual.

'It's cool,' Spencer says, but realises that he's sweating. He takes this as an effect of his father's scrutiny rather than the cop's. Or it might be a symptom of his own ill health. He resolves that when he gets back to London he will improve his diet and his body. Take walks and bicycle rides. Maybe even join a gym and face the self-ridicule of working out. Sit sweating healthy sweat on a rowing machine watching share prices tumble on a TV set.

'How do you like them apples?' Spencer says. He tries to remember some of his father's other catchphrases. When his father was in his difficult, combative prime, he had accumulated a small batch of phrases that he would recite at moments he thought were appropriate in order to demonstrate his unimpeachable ordinary Americanness.

'You'll be the only boy in the girls' school,' Spencer says. 'Piss or get off the pot. That'll put hair on your chest . . . from the inside!'

'When they made you . . .' his father starts to say.

And Spencer nods in his sentimentality, hoping his father will get to some former coherency even if it is an entirely fatuous one.

But his father doesn't reach it—the sentence dribbles away into the awkward vacuum where most of his conversation resides.

The patrol car that had been beside them speeds away, looking for more dangerous company.

'What's your favourite music?' Spencer says.

'Absolutely,' his father says, which is his customary remark when he is not sure what is required of him in a conversation.

'Your favourite songs,' Spencer persists. 'Or artists. Singers. You liked Frank Sinatra didn't you?'

'Sure,' his father expansively says.

'We could get some Sinatra on the soundtrack, but it might be a bit cutesy-cutesy. On the nose, if you know what I mean. It might also cost a lot.'

'Dime a dozen.'

Spencer tries the radio. He finds jazz on NPR, which gives a nice atmospheric soundtrack to their drive, but his father reaches down irritably to fidget and fumble with the radio buttons, so Spencer switches it off again.

'When are we seeing Gribitz?' Spencer's father says. 'I haven't been able to shit for a week.'

'We saw him. We saw him today,' Spencer reminds him.

'Who?' Spencer's father says.

His father had been a strong man, the smartest and toughest man Spencer had ever known. He feels the loss of his own vitality and cohesion more painfully even than Spencer does, more than anyone except, probably, his wife, whom he now rejects because she condemns him for his weakness. It is painful to be in his company now, diminished, incoherent, uncohesive. It is as if pieces of him have been allowed to drift in different directions, untethered. Spencer feels an enormous rush of pity and shame, which is abruptly halted when Spencer's father asks him,

'How's your friend doing? The flower guy.'

Spencer despises and envies his more successful contemporaries and friends. He has kept true to an ethos derived from high modernism and trash pop and has no time for anything that smacks of sentimentality or *storytelling*. Films are art and they are garbage and he disparages anything that aims for the in-between. He has seen the cleverest animator of his acquaintance, who had made beautiful suprematist miniatures that rigorously separated themselves from reference and representation, make a fortune from TV commercials and, ultimately, Hollywood. Others had become hacks, others had given up on the form and, or (or both), on themselves. Spencer had stuck to it. We admire your bravery, his friends tell him. Spencer had long ago realised that when people say *brave* they usually mean *stupid*.

'Who's the flower guy?' Spencer asks, when he knows perfectly well who his father means.

'You know. Nick. Dick. The one with all the write-ups in the *Times*.'

'Nick? I can't think of who you mean.'

'Ah. Forget about it.'

'The point about the movies,' Spencer says, 'is that what everyone wants is an idea that can be summed up in one line, or less. The pioneer was *Twins*. People still talk about that with reverence. *Arnold Schwarzenegger and Danny DeVito are twins!* You've got the idea, you've got the stars, you've got the poster, it's all there, in one dumb-stupid sentence.'

'Schwarzenegger, yeah. She's good.'

'I happen to think,' Spencer says, with a pomposity that sounds awful to his own ears, 'that if a film can be summed up in one sentence then there really isn't much point to making it. Why bother?'

The lies that movie cameras tell, that the field of vision is as exclusive as the shape of a frame, that no one feels pain, that everything is surface, that things can make sense.

'What's the point of making a film if it's not going to change the world?' Spencer says.

'Maybe because people enjoy it?'

Sometimes, still, his father can summon up a difficult acuity. Spencer responds by being merciful.

'Rick Violet. That's who you're asking about.'

'That's right. You still not talking?'

The last time that Spencer and Rick Violet had fallen out was when they were each surprisingly featured in a news-paper's end-of-year round-up opining as to the five best films of the year. Spencer was seldom asked to do this kind of thing; Rick seldom agreed to it. Rick was not featured on Spencer's list, which he had tried to compile scrupulously, and then lost the list he was making and forgot the spellings

of the directors' names and had to improvise on the phone
to a subeditor.

Rick's choices had been shrewdly advised. The reason that
Spencer took offence was that his own most recent film was
on the list, and its selection could have been made because
Rick's shrewd adviser wanted something that could qualify as
an obscure gem that hardly anyone would have heard of, or
Rick himself had included it as an act of patronising generosity,
and Spencer couldn't decide which was more odious.

'No. Well yeah, we're sort of friends again.'

Shamefully, a week before his departure from London, he
had called Rick Violet. Spencer had been running bad online,
his Visa card was just above its maximum, and there was enough
money left in his overdraft to pay either his rent or buy flights
and rent a New York hotel room for three days. The Short Beach
Film Festival would offer him hospitality in Atlantic City but
was not able to pay for him to get there. They assured him that
he would understand. The only four people in the world who
would give him the money he needed were the last people he
would want to ask—his father, his producer, his almost ex-wife,
and Rick Violet.

Just to test the water, he told himself, when in truth it was
to toy with humiliation and shame, to taunt himself with his
own feelings of inadequacy and dependence, he called up
Rick, because he was the one he liked the least of the four.
An assistant answered the phone, as an assistant always did.
Rick's assistants were invariably women, invariably beautiful,
invariably in love with Rick. The only variety was the identity of the assistant; over the past few years, Spencer had
never seen or spoken to the same woman twice. He left a
message that he'd called, and a few hours later Rick was on
the line.

'I'm having a little party. It would be great if you could come,'
Spencer had said.

'Birthday?'

'No, just a party. No particular occasion. You know, drinks, people, maybe show some movies. It's safe, I won't be showing any of mine.'

'Hey. *Compadre*. I love your movies. You know I'm your number-one fan.'

This wasn't entirely false. Complacent in the knowledge that he was fabulously successful and Spencer a hardly-heard-of purist, Rick could indulge and patronise and, it was true, appreciate Spencer's work, which made it all the more galling.

'Yes, well, likewise,' Spencer said. 'It would be nice if you could make it.'

'That's so sweet of you. I'll be there.'

It was a safe invitation. There was no chance that Rick would attend a party of Spencer's, even if he were actually hosting one.

The conversation would move, as Spencer knew it was destined to, on to Rick's casually worn glory. First, though, as if interested, Rick asked Spencer how things were in his world.

'Oh. You know. A little rough. Trying to raise some money.'

'You know you can count on me for contributions. You know that.'

'I know that, Rick. I know.'

One of the subsidiary agonies of talking to Rick was the effect it had on Spencer's speech patterns. He adopted the bogus style of dialogue of a character in one of Rick's own awful films, reiterating vaguely significant phrases, calling Rick repeatedly by his name.

This was it now, when he might ask, state a figure that Rick would enjoy rounding up to the nearest five thousand. He could hear in the silence of the telephone Rick's offer of charity waiting—well, not exactly silence, a hubbub of activity, people talking on telephones, carrying things, the industrial whirl of Rick's success.

'Tell me, how's it all going with you, Rick?'

And here it would come, the litany of triumphs, the different projects on the go, most of it glossed over as if it was annoying, Spencer would understand, as few people could, the pain of the incidental, when all Rick wanted, all he ever wanted, was to make movies. And then, in the midst of this, one clunking moment—just when Spencer would be feeling that maybe he was too hard on Rick, that Abbie and all the others could be right, that Rick was a nice guy, who had talent, so why begrudge him any of his luck?—he would drop into the conversation something so tactlessly self-regarding that at least one positive effect of their conversation would be that Spencer would be supported in his resentments and spites.

'It's good, it's good.' Rick had been saying something about a recent triumph in a festival that Spencer had never been invited to, but was now segueing into a topic that he expected Spencer to be familiar with. 'But you've probably been following all this, I shouldn't bore you with it again.'

'Well I've been busy. I'm off to a festival shortly myself.'

'Cannes? I'm getting kind of tired of that. But I guess I'll probably see you there. You in competition? Or *Un Certain Regard*?'

Rick's French accent was casually, affectedly poor, with just a few glimpses of its available perfection.

'Uh, no. Not Cannes. America.'

'Oh, Ann Arbor. I love that festival. A lot of people don't get how cool it is.'

'Um. No. East Coast.'

'Well that's great, Spence. Terrific. I didn't even know there was a festival going on there right now. But that commercial of yours must have opened up a lot of doors.'

'What commercial?'

'Yeah yeah. Heh. Right. Anyway. I was saying. You must have heard about the Oscar shenanigans.'

'No, Rick. I don't think I have.'

'Really? There's been coverage in the dailies and the trade of course.'

'Never buy them.'

'Well who would unless they had to, Spence?' (This was another habit of Rick's, to establish some kind of intimacy with whoever he was talking to by settling upon some unpleasant diminutive of their name.) 'Word up. I hear you. But online?'

'Nope.' (He didn't know why he was making such a point of this, except as a futile attempt to deny Rick something he wanted.)

'You mean you never Google me?'

This was said in naked, startled disbelief.

'Never have, Rick, never have,' Spencer said, but of course he has, he does it a lot; the last time, the evening before, he had learned that Rick had recently been made a Chevalier de l'Ordre des Artes et des Lettres, which had irked Spencer beyond speech and postponed this telephone call by a day.

After he had managed to end the conversation without asking for any money, Spencer transferred his remaining funds into his DiamondPoker account and played for four and a half hours, in which time he successfully channelled his sickly fury to quadruple his starting stake, and had enough cash to pay both his rent and his New York expenses.

Spencer's mobile telephone rings, to his father's irritation. Jimmy Ludwig does not like competition or rivalry for attention. It is Mary, who is sobbing.

'Daddy. Daddy,' she says.

'Hey honey.'

'Daddy, I'm sorry I said you were rubbish. You're not rubbish. You're nice and pretty and I love you. I didn't mean it.'

'It's OK, I know you didn't mean it.'

'Did you?'

She marvels at this.

'How could you?' she asks. '*I* didn't know that.'

'Look. I better go. I'm driving.'

'I love you Daddy.'

These are beautiful words, and just as he counts on Mary eventually to forgive him all his derelictions and failures, so too he will forgive her anything so long as she remembers to speak this sentence.

'That was Mary,' he says.

His father is sulking now, looking glumly at the drying damp patch on his groin, fiddling with his surgical collar.

'You shouldn't take that off.'

His father ignores him, continues to pull at the Velcro fastening, and Spencer catches an unwelcome sympathy for how his stepmother must feel.

'You should keep that on,' Spencer says.

'Should I?'

'Yes. It's for the best.'

His father dutifully refastens his collar and looks so grateful for the attention that Spencer's heart is pierced. And he is so confused by this feeling that he answers his telephone without looking to check the identity of the caller.

'Spencer!'

'Oh. Right. Hi Michelle.'

'Spencer!'

'Hi.'

'Where have you been hiding yourself?'

'Not hiding. I'm in the States.'

'Oh. Your *father*. How *is* he?'

Michelle's voice drops. She is attentive and kind and wise, alert always to nuances of emotion and need, and Spencer has come to hate his dependency upon her. He owes her money. She will have a job that she thinks he ought to take, and not because she is looking for repayment, but because she approves of the project and she hopes, she has always hoped, that it will bring out the best in him. Michelle has been unyielding in her support for Spencer over the years. Spencer and Michelle co-produce his films. This is because he is prone to making the self-damaging, heartfelt decision. He gets things wrong. He finds it hard to take many people seriously, particularly money men, and he hates indulging others while being patronised by them. Michelle does these things for him.

He knows he is an unrewarding colleague. He takes things as his due, without consideration. She has other people she works with, other, better, jobs that she will be prepared to sacrifice to further his work. The understanding among their friends is that she is unspokenly in love with him, but neither Spencer nor Michelle believe this to be true. If he is actually ever to make *it, the* Film by Spencer Ludwig, then he will have to be free to make it, which means he will have to be free of all obligation. Michelle will have to be paid off before they can work together again. Spencer has decided that if his life is to go in any manageable way then he has to sunder all links of dependency.

His father is sulking again. He defiantly removes his surgical collar and places it in his lap.

'Look. Michelle. I'm driving right now. I'll call you as soon as I can.'

'Please do. I've got some great news for you. Don't you want to hear it? Maybe it's what you need. You sound quite down.'

'It had better wait. I'm sorry.'

His father is now looking at his own cellphone, which his wife has insisted he carry with him at all times. He seldom switches it on, because his wife will always be calling him on it. But he switches it on now and Spencer can see that there are seven unanswered calls, all from what might be bitterly called home.

'I'll call you as soon as I can. Sorry Michelle.'

He switches the phone off and tosses it on to the dashboard. 'Sorry,' he says to his father. 'That was my producer.'

His father grunts, and tosses his own phone to join Spencer's.

They are driving along the West Side now, parallel to the Hudson. Across the river is New Jersey, where Spencer was born, and which he was delighted to escape. He could turn around now, deliver his father back to his world, but he is not going to do that.

What is this for? It is for Spencer's father. Living in a world without pleasure or curiosity or joy is no life at all. Spencer's father spends his crepuscular time between doctors' appointments solving jigsaw puzzles. In the corner of the living room that his wife had wanted to exile him from is where he was accustomed to read the newspaper in the morning and where now he is accustomed to sit with the newspaper in the morning and mimic his former habits and pursuits. His short-term memory was damaged by the stroke. By the time he has begun the second paragraph of a news item, his fractured memory has lost anything of what was in the first.

'We're going to Atlantic City. We shall have fun,' Spencer says.

Spencer imagines walks along the ocean, soft exchanges of secrets in plush congenial bars, rich widows and Russian heiresses decorously offering their attentions, as father and son light up Cuban cigars. But Spencer's father gave up smoking when he was fifty. He used to smoke three or four packs a day, light the next cigarette from the embers of the previous one, or start another when the current cigarette was still alight in the ashtray. To sit on his father's lap was a desired pleasure but not painless. Spencer learnt early it was best to dress for the occasion; to dress as an American child, in shorts and short-sleeved shirts, was asking for trouble, the burning ash dropping from his father's mouth and hand on to his unprotected skin.

A last hurrah, the desperados make one final ride-out. Or maybe this is the first of many, one long trip, the first chapter from New York to Atlantic City, and then farther, Route 66, through the desert, Las Vegas, Los Angeles, down to Mexico, Spencer and his father on the road, and no matter how jeopardising this might be for his health, it must be good to feel the air on his face—Spencer insists, on this subject he is intractable, unbullyable, that they have the windows down rather than use the Cadillac's air conditioning—the experience of speed in itself is a good thing.

Spencer's father needs his son to make this happen. He takes a solidity in the presence of his son, it is some kind of connection to a world that goes on living, a world that he once was a significant part of.

And what does Spencer want from this? Can he still take a solidifying comfort in the substance of his father?

As they drive through lower Manhattan, Spencer is gratified to see there are more homeless people on the streets than there used to be. If his father is going to die he wants, vengefully, to see systems crumble.

'How much?' his father says.

'How much what?'

The Lincoln Tunnel was always Spencer's less-preferred. He loves the Holland Tunnel best, the sheer length of it, the railed platform along the side where policemen used to stand and slowly wave back to Spencer, helpless and besotted in the back seat. He felt ridiculous waving to policemen, even when he was eight or nine years old and taking trips with his father and stepmother, but he couldn't help himself, there was an unavoidable exhilaration about it.

'Your . . . judgement.'

His father knows he has said the wrong word and retreats into an abashed tunnel-darkened silence. Spencer's policy on matters of this kind is to push him, so his father won't settle into an accustomed lonely space behind walls of ununderstood language.

'My, what?'

'Judgement. I want to . . .'

In the darkness of the tunnel, his father, still expert in matters such as these, retrieves his wallet from the back pocket of his chinos, picks out from behind his Medicare and AARP cards the loose cheque that he keeps for emergencies.

'Pay?'

'Right.'

'There's toll booths on the Turnpike, but I've got cash. They don't take cheques.'

'No. Your . . .' His father makes a forlorn effort of concentration, shakes his head. 'It's pathetic,' he says.

They are into New Jersey now, dipping up out of the tunnel into the glare of a less glamorous light. The road takes one regretful curve towards and then away from the Manhattan skyline and they are in the state where Spencer was born, forty-odd years ago, where he had learned to speak with an American accent at kindergarten and first grade, because otherwise he would stick out more than he already did, his sensitive ways, his take on the world, his incapacity for roughhousing with older, more athletic boys, and with an English accent at home, because his mother disapproved of all aspects of America.

Spencer's notional best friend when he was six wanted to become a policeman, because policemen carry guns. A few months ago, trying to explain to his daughter who he was or at least who he had been and what he might have been in danger of becoming, he had told her about his early years in New Jersey and Mary had insisted on looking up the name of his notional best friend on Google. Raymond Auch still lived in Berkeley Heights. He had not become a policeman. He was a senior vice-president in his father's real estate firm and had married well, into a blue-blood family from Philadelphia. Mary had found the wedding announcement on the *New York Times* site. Spencer always told people that if he had stayed in New Jersey he would probably have become a junkie or a lawyer or both.

His mother disapproved of chewing gum and television, instant coffee, big cars, what the country had allowed her husband to be, who he insisted on becoming. In the cold rigour of mealtimes, the three of them sat uncomfortably together, each not being able quite to comprehend how this was his or her world, where nothing, to any of them, ever seemed entirely familiar.

Spencer as a child—he made up for it subsequently—ate very slowly, to his father's irritation and disapproval. His mother, in sympathetic complicity, would give smaller and smaller portions each time, which he would halve with his knife, and when he had laboured to consume the first half, he would halve the remainder again, and so on, in an infinite progression.

But this is not meant to be a memory drive.

'No, go on. What are you trying to say?' Spencer says.

'It's pathetic,' his father repeats.

'My judgement?'

'Not judgement. Journey.'

His father settles back, looking first pleased with himself and then angry that selecting and finding the right word to express his thought should be such a source of pride.

'Journey? You mean my plane ticket?'

'That's right.'

'You don't have to do that. I'm not asking you for the money.'

'I know you're not.'

Which is why, probably, he is prepared to give it. Spencer had learned, not long after leaving New Jersey, that any money he accepted from his father was a lever of power he was voluntarily submitting himself to. He had made it a policy after that never to ask for money from his father and seldom to accept it when it was offered.

'It was six hundred dollars. Approximately.'

His father now looks for a pen.

'Why don't you wait until we stop somewhere. We'll need to stop somewhere for lunch and gasoline.'

'I want a . . . a . . .'

'Pen?'

His father spreads his arms out wide in his ignominy, touching the window with his right hand, the gear stick with his left.

Pylons surround their road. Spencer manages to drive one-handed and take a photograph of a line of them. Spencer finds pylons magnificent.

'There's one in the glove compartment,' Spencer says, and he returns his phone to its perch above the dashboard and reaches over to wave towards the glove compartment.

Rather ingeniously, Spencer's father uses the glove compartment door as a writing desk. He concentrates hard on forming the words, puffing out his cheeks as he carefully writes, before signing it with a flourish. He examines what he has made and hands the cheque over to Spencer, who has to struggle to take it while passing a truck that has lumbered on to the road from a strip of low-slung no-tell motels. (Air-Conditioning In Every Room! Free HBO! Daily And Weekly Rates. Mirrored Rooms Available!)

Spencer interprets his father's assiduousness in trying to pay his son's expenses as a way to expressing who might still be in charge, and also, maybe, if he offers to pay this then he won't have to pay more.

'Thank you,' Spencer says.

'You're welcome,' his father says.

If he were to make this journey into a film, Spencer would resist the too-obvious irony of the self-professed Garden State being a jumble of pylons and factory chimneys and desperate stunted occasional trees trying to make their leafless lives between iron bridges and car parks. Instead he might chart the journey in its road signs, exits to Jersey City, the Holland Tunnel, Bayonne, Newark Airport, Elizabeth, Elizabeth Seaport, the Verazzano Bridge. Improbably and unpersuasively, a billboard, half hidden behind a gas tower, tries to inform them that they are in The Embroidery Capital Of The World! He doesn't see any signs for Atlantic City, which worries him.

'What was the scenery like when you were growing up?'

'What's that?'

'The countryside. When you were a boy?'

'In Poland? It was beautiful.'

His father sometimes permits himself to become sentimental about his childhood. It is a tactic that Spencer allows himself on occasion, to question his father about his youth in Warsaw. While his father's memory has grown unreliable about recent events, it is sure on the distant past. And sometimes he will talk about the taste of pickles in brine when he and his friend Benny broke into the cucumber factory at night, or the fresh buttered bagels you could buy on the innocently pre-War street—or not so innocent: his father could also tell stories about the gangs of Polish youths who roamed the streets, whose ideal recreation was to find Jews to beat up. His father, this wasting-away man, who was fastidious with his Italian suits and restaurant cutlery (even if every suit of clothes wore a reminder of the meal he had just eaten), who had made himself at home in law courts and yacht clubs, had taken to carrying a bicycle chain wherever he went. On at least one occasion he had used it, slashing iron across the face of a teenaged Pole, whose cap he had taken away as a souvenir. One victory among many defeats, he had told Spencer.

'Did you go to the water ever?'

'Sure,' his father says. 'The lakes. In summer.'

'All of you?'

'Me, my brother and my mother. And some cousins. We rented a house on the water.'

'Not your father?'

'He was working.'

A tradition that Spencer's father's father had probably inherited from his own father—pack off the family to the lakes for the summer, while he stayed in the city to swelter and work and pursue whatever recreations grass-widowed men find to occupy themselves. Spencer's father had followed the same tradition—in the time that Spencer had lived with both his parents, all his holidays were taken with his mother, flying back to England to join the company of her married, unchilded, older sister in dusty guest houses on the South Coast, Hastings, Bournemouth, Weston-super-Mare. And Spencer followed it too: he had never understood the notion of a family holiday; even in the happiest times with Mary and her mother, he had always resisted summers in Walberswick and Tuscany.

Exit 11 offers them the Amboys, Shore Point and the Garden State Parkway, North and South.

'*The Secret Life of Walter Mitty*, that's where he lived, Perth Amboy,' Spencer says.

'Left!' says his father.

'You remember? Danny Kaye was in it.'

'Left! Left!' wails his father.

'You used to like Danny Kaye. You remember him?'

'For crying out loud!'

And his father grinds his dentures and reaches to grab for the wheel, and Spencer accepts the situation is an urgent one.

'Oh. I get it. The Parkway? Which direction?'

'North, sure. Why not? The same way we came,' his father says, gaining articulacy through derision.

Spencer twists the wheel to the right, a triumph of bravado and fear, forces the Cadillac across the bows of an aged Toyota pick-up, and steers-veers the car into the exit lane.

He quietens his heart as he pays the toll to get on to the Garden State Parkway.

'I need a leak,' his father says.

All the rest stops, or at least the two that Spencer misses, timid again at the wheel of his father's car, unwilling or unable to force a way through the traffic to get to the exit lane, are named for US presidents. He drives past, to his father's woe, the Jefferson rest stop and then the Reagan.

'I need a fucking leak! Why are you so dawdle?!'

Spencer eases the car into the slow lane, hunkers over the wheel; he is not going to miss the next exit.

Pulling, finally, into the car park of the pleasingly named Cheesequake Service Area rest stop, Spencer has hardly brought the car to a halt when his father has opened the passenger door and is already setting off for the journey across the tarmac past pick-up trucks and sedans, dragging his oxygen cylinder behind him. Spencer hurriedly secures the car and catches up with his father, who is walking at an impressive pace, arms behind his back, his right hand clutching his withered left wrist, his head down, chin to chest, his eyes glancing up from time to time to check on his direction. Spencer takes hold of the cylinder, opens the door to the rest stop.

'Do you think there was a President Cheesequake? I don't remember him.'

'What are you talking about?'

'Just trying to take your mind off your bladder.'

His father moves faster and shakes him off at the men's-room door. Spencer hooks the oxygen cylinder over his father's arm and waits for him in the corridor outside.

He looks at the cheque for the first time. The figure matches the correctly spelled words, which doesn't always happen in the accounting system of his father's decline. Except: his father has made the amount out for six thousand dollars instead of six hundred.

'It's too much,' he says, showing the cheque to his father upon his unsteady return from the men's room.

Spencer tries to return the cheque but his father waves it away. He rests for a moment, to gather strength, on the plastic saddle of a mechanical horse that would cost fifty cents to gently rock a child into amusement, before he dourly gets on with the business of wavering towards the café area.

'Very generous, thank you,' Spencer says.

He quickly folds the cheque away, as if there were something shameful about it, into the breast pocket of his jacket. Maybe he will keep it as a souvenir, the ironic symbol of the near-possibility of parental help.

Jimmy Ludwig ignores the woman who offers to steer him towards a table. He finds one himself, lowers himself bumpily into a chair and rests his arms expectantly on the Formica tabletop.

'OK. Let's go to work.'

'The backgammon? I left it in the car.'

His father purses his lips. His son has disappointed him, again.

Spencer goes back to the car, retrieves the backgammon set and hesitates for a moment, because he has left the cellphones inside, clearly displayed on the shelf above the glove compartment, then hesitates for a second moment because he has parked the Cadillac, inexpertly, across two bays that are reserved for buses; but there are three stretch limousines parked there too, and a police car, New Jersey State Trooper, beside an Academy bus that announces cheerily that it is an Atlantic City Casino Special!

'No,' he says out loud, alarming the line of passengers descending from the bus, most of whom are old, most of whom look poor, all of whom snake away from him.

A few still slumber in the rear seats, faces uncomfortable against the window. He says NO! again, louder this time. He will take this at least from his father, that this is his world and he shall do what he likes.

His father is waiting impatiently in the centre of the eating area. Spencer wonders whether he would pick him out even if he didn't know him. His father's pastel-yellow short-sleeved shirt, white windcheater, beige chinos, the large nose and small eyes that can barely contain so much impatience and quiet fury; and Spencer's burdened heart lifts with love and tenderness for the old man who used, once, to terrify him into tears and a sense of the difficulty, perhaps futility, of accomplishing anything meaningful in the world.

'Well what do you want? They have burgers, pizzas and, uh, yogurt, by the looks of things.'

His father shrugs. He's not listening, and he doesn't care. Even if President Cheesequake himself offered him a pickled cucumber dripping brine and a buttered bagel from the Warsaw streets circa 1939, Spencer's father would not care. Food is a burden, forced upon him by his wife and now his son.

'Let's get to work,' his father says, and opens up the backgammon set.

'I'm going to have a burger. Do you want a burger?'

'Whatever you like, I'm not tired,' his father says.

Spencer orders cheeseburgers for them both, medium rare, and cups of coffee. When the waitress returns with the coffees, his father, ungraciously, grabs his cup off her tray.

'Where's the . . .?'

'That's mine. Yours has got milk.'

'That'll put hairs on your chest,' Spencer's father says. 'From the inside.'

He holds out three pink packets of Sweet 'n' Lo, which has become an unspoken ritual between them. Spencer's father has hardly any strength left in his hands. He is unable to tie his shoelaces or button up his shirts or behead the packets of sweetener he laces his coffee with. Spencer twists off the tops of the packets, and Spencer's father nods, both in gratitude and as a kind of statement of the dry banal horror his life has become reduced to.

As they wait for their food, they play backgammon. When their food arrives his father sulks, because he has just won two games in a row and resents the break in their sport.

Spencer eats in a kind of voluptuous joy. He had not realised how hungry he was. His father eats more or less effectively. Spencer suspects that his father has no sense of smell and little sense of taste. Spencer's father is accustomed to two meals; Spencer likes to eat at least three or four times a day. It never occurs to his father and it never has that anyone else might be feeling something different to him. *You have no empathy*, Spencer had once told his father. *You remind me of your mother*, Spencer's father had said in reply, which was not a statement of approval.

When he was a child and stayed with his father and step-mother, Spencer's appetite was always being confounded. He spent the days either hungry or overstuffed from the monstrous dinners that Spencer's stepmother provided. It never occurred to either adult that the child might be hungry, and Spencer had found it always difficult to express his desires in his father's and stepmother's world.

'How is it?'

His father makes a doleful face. It is the expression he uses when he is asked how he slept, when an elevator man asks him how he is feeling, when he deigns to look at his wife when she is talking.

'You want to try some?'

'No. No thank you. Here. Try some of mine.'

The doleful face becomes brutal in its contempt. Spencer is grateful for the return of the waitress. Despite his protestations of hungerlessness, Spencer's father consumes his cheeseburger, with only a few dots of mustard and ketchup on his trousers and shirt to show for it. He pushes away the plates, which

Spencer is about to dispose of, but is deterred by his father opening up the backgammon set again.

'Let's get to work,' his father says.

The set is an old wooden one, bought at least thirty years before, when the smart thing among affluent co-dependent New York couples was to play backgammon. Mr and Mrs Jimmy Ludwig had followed the pursuits appropriate to their age and station and class. They had taken up, and soon abandoned, golf and then tennis. For two years they had season tickets at Madison Square Garden for New York Rangers ice hockey games. For six months, they became devotees of Transcendental Meditation. They had travelled, safari in South Africa, tours of South-East Asian Buddhist temples. But the only thing that had really taken with Spencer's father was yachting. He loved piloting his boat, tinkering around in its engine room, the pre-attorney engineer at home in the oil and the machinery and the grease. When Spencer stayed with his father and stepmother during his desolate American childhood summers, he had sat on the boat, moored on the Long Island Sound, and watched his father and stepmother play backgammon on this board. It had been made by Gucci, the points were green and red triangles, and all the pieces had the Gucci symbol etched in gold, which now had faded. One of the pieces had been lost and been replaced by a smaller, unmarked disc from another set. One of Spencer's few achievements in his father's eyes was that he had supplanted his stepmother as the preferred opponent.

After a while, Spencer forgets what kind of spectacle they must be offering. This would be a scene he would have in his movie, father and son, the schlump and the dying man, sitting at a Formica table with a backgammon board between them, bright lights, a black plastic condiment stand holding mustards and ketchup, another with sachets of sugar and Sweet 'n' Lo, a salt and pepper shaker, uncomprehending men in baseball caps at nearby tables, the looks of pity and fear that pass between them when they look at the old man with his oxygen tank. And the action, the click-clacking of dice rolling on the wooden board, the movement of the pieces, sliding and grazing and sometimes slamming down on their points.

His father hates to lose, at anything, especially at backgammon against his son. Not only is he a bad loser, he is also a terrible winner. Spencer lets him take the first couple of after-lunch boards, and the glee with which his father watches Spencer write down the points he's gained is unseemly. He complains when Spencer throws a double, but when Spencer draws attention to his father throwing two doubles in a row, his father gloats.

'Ah, stop crying,' his father says.

And Spencer sets out to play as well as he can.

'Incredible,' his father says when Spencer makes a long-range hit on an exposed piece.

'Disgusting,' his father says when Spencer throws a double five to escape his home-board trap.

When Jimmy Ludwig plays backgammon, he is in accord with a part of his brain that has been untouched by strokes and aphasia and death. He sees the position clearly, chooses the correct—and biggest—play instantly. If there is a choice between a dull safe move and a hit of one of Spencer's pieces, then he will always make the hit, even if it leaves him exposed in his home board. And his language is untroubled. There is a kind of deliverance in the pursuit, except it is gruelling to be part of the nakedness of his father's need to win. It is the only aspect of his life that, as far as Spencer is aware, still holds any pleasure for him, or urgency.

And meanwhile Spencer is streaking along a run of luck. He even executes a Coup Classique. His father had borne off all but three of his pieces while Spencer kept one man back on the farthest-away point of his father's home board while building a fortification on his own. Spencer has one chance to hit, and takes it. His father takes an age to return to the board and by the time he has done so, Spencer is about to win the game.

Both Spencer and his father are grateful when the waitress returns to clear away the debris of their food.

'Can I interest you gentlemen in some dessert?'

'Sure,' his father says.

'You having something?' Spencer says.

'Not for me. You go ahead. More tea.'

'He means coffee,' Spencer says.

'And the check.'

'You got it. And for you, sir?'

His father reaches into his wallet for his American Express card, which he waves towards Spencer.

'It's OK, it's on me,' Spencer says.

'Sir?'

Spencer reckons that he has been called *sir* today more than he ever has been. He wonders where this will end. He feels obliged to order a dessert. Even though he will make unkind remarks about Spencer's eating habits and weight, it gives his father a peculiar kind of pleasure, perhaps fatherly in nature, to sit impatient while his son consumes mounds of sweet stuff in public.

Chapter Three

Spencer's stepmother has called them three times on his father's cellphone and twice on Spencer's. He has also missed calls from Mary and Michelle. He sees the list of calls missed when they return to the car.

'Where are we going? Gribitz?' Spencer's father says.

'No. Atlantic City.'

'Why?'

'Film festival. I told you. I've been invited. I'll be giving an interview, and there'll be some screenings—they seem to want to hold a retrospective of my work—and there'll be a dinner, a gala dinner.'

His father seems impressed, and maybe proud, which is rare.

'Your plays?'

'Yes. My films.'

The Academy bus from the Cheesequake car park is ahead and Spencer accelerates to catch up and then settle in behind it. Despite the derision and contempt he will receive for driving so slowly, this is less nerve-racking than relying on his father's sense of direction.

His father's cellphone rings again. Spencer reaches to answer it but Jimmy beats him to it. With a speed and a sureness that are admirable given his state and age, Spencer's father grabs hold of the cellphone with his left hand and stabs his window open with his right and all of it in one fluidly jerky action throws the phone spiralling out of the car to the side of the road and stabs the window shut again and sits back, grimly triumphant.

Spencer quickly takes hold of his own phone and slips it for safety into the breast pocket of his jacket. It beeps and vibrates busily against his chest.

'Let me have a look of that.'

'Why?'

'Let me have a look.'

Reluctantly, Spencer passes over his telephone. His father sneers at it while lowering the window.

'Please. No,' Spencer says.

His father smiles.

'I need that,' Spencer says. 'Work.'

'Keep your eyes on the road.'

It is good advice; Spencer has been wavering the car out of its lane. He is almost touching the bus with its cargo of sleeping old women and small men in hats whose heads hardly reach the oval bus windows.

His father's aim is true. When he has restored the car to its lane, Spencer looks in the mirror to see his mobile telephone skittering, bouncing and breaking on the gravel behind them.

There is no way back. Spencer is driving in the middle lane. There are cars behind and on either side. His telephone is irretrievable. They can only go further.

After Cheesequake, nature. The Parkway cuts through townships, well-mannered white wooden houses, American flags fluttering in front of civic buildings. They drive past forests, where sturdy blond outdoor types hike along narrow creeks through the pine trees.

'It's a different ecosystem here,' Spencer says. 'Garden state.'

But his father is sleeping, exhausted after his latest triumph. His mouth is open, lower lip trembling; he is lightly snoring.

Spencer has to be careful not to do what he used to do, years ago, on American road trips with his father, before his father trusted him to drive better than he trusted himself. Spencer would gaze half hypnotised at the broken white lines in the middle of the road, the grey unbroken concrete slab of the median divide, and make shapes and faces and sleepily troubling meanings out of the blur.

'Vertigo,' Spencer says, 'is much misunderstood. It's not a fear of heights, it's a desire to throw yourself off them.'

A car horn hoots, he pulls the Cadillac back into lane and a fist waves at him through the window of a red pick-up truck that speeds past them on their left.

His father sleeps on, undisturbed, untroubled, except for the inadequate volume of oxygen his hopeless diaphragm can draw into his thirsty lungs. Spencer wipes the sweat away from his brow and turns on the radio, keeping the sound down. He follows the Academy bus and listens to jazz on NPR.

'This,' says Spencer, looking at his sleeping father, thrilled and frightened at the starkness of the thought and at the audacity of speaking it out loud, 'is a film to finish before you die.'

Driving along the Parkway looking through the windscreen of the Cadillac derealises everything. The world is two-dimensional, nothing is quite alive. Spencer's urge to twist the wheel is not just a rebellion against enforced orderliness, the tyranny of straight lines, or even the vertiginous thrill of yielding, of softness longing for hardness, the consummation of collision, it is also a desire to connect, to make human contact, even in the messiness of blood and broken flesh.

Spencer did not do nature, he did people, and things. Not for him the speedy dissolves of clouds rolling over a huge blue sky. If he had a camera with him, he would have filmed the rest-stop restaurant scene in Cheesequake, the Coup Classique, his father's face, the apartment day-bed/toaster-oven debates, his stepmother's face, some shots of the road, the first elevated section of the New Jersey Turnpike, big ten-wheelers, the toll booth in the rain, he'd hire a policeman to slowly wave to them in the Lincoln Tunnel, he'd film the factories and pylons and smokestacks they pass by.

And the footage would be linked and voice-overed by Spencer's voice. He has narrated films before and he makes a fair enough job of it. His voice is low, considered, a little wheezy. It would get its premiere at the Navarra Film Festival or maybe Toronto, be bought by Channel 4 and PSB. And the whole thing would be utterly predictable. Pathos, poignancy, the Atlantic City School. He is glad not to have a camera with him.

The work that he is proudest of—*Robert W's Last Walk, The Captain's Grief*—is the work that the world has most disregarded. The novelties and fripperies—*One Door Opens*, *Competition*—are the ones that do best. There is a message here, but Spencer chooses not to hear it. He feels that in some way he is being rewarded, or punished, for his least important work. It could only be worse if the world paid him its greatest respect for the films he hasn't even made.

Spencer's early ambition, still as unrealised as the world through a car windscreen, was to show pain. Film is good at showing actors' vanity. Brando in the dust at Karl Malden's boots. When Joan of Arc is tortured she shows ecstasy.

His father is in pain even in sleep. Except it does not quite reveal itself in the little intermittent winces at the corners of his mouth; the irritated movements show themselves as irritation merely. So how does Spencer feel his father's pain? It is an act of empathy that film surely must be capable of mediating.

'It can't be surface only,' Spencer says. 'Or maybe it is.'

'What's that?'

His father snaps to wakefulness.

'I was just thinking,' Spencer says. 'How you feeling? You hurting? I've often thought, or sometimes at any rate, that there must be some internal compensation to getting older. Is there?'

'I don't understand what you're saying.'

A narrow stripe of white that looks like forgotten toothpaste is etched into the line that cuts his father's face from the corner of his mouth to his chin.

'When you get older, does the system adjust? Balance out somehow? I mean, is it like someone going blind? You know, suddenly their other senses get more acute? They can hear better than they ever could before? That sort of thing.'

'I don't get what you're saying.'

This might be answer in itself, but Spencer persists,

'Maybe something internal, dream life or some such. Natural opiates. Autoeroticism. Happy memories of childhood. The body gets worse, the mind compensates.'

'Is there anything good about getting old? Is that what you're asking?'

'Yes. That's right.'

'I don't buy that. It's all shit,' Spencer's father says.

'Right. OK. But isn't there *anything*? Anything at all that gets better?'

'I'll tell you. This is how it is,' Spencer's father says.

He slams his right hand down on the glove compartment, maybe for emphasis, maybe because he doesn't have any better control of his movements. With his index finger he traces a diagonal line up to the right.

'Child,' Spencer's father says.

The line then goes horizontal some way towards the passenger door.

'This is . . .?' Spencer's father looks to him for the word.

'Man's estate.'

'What?'

'Adult. Grown-up? Man.'

'Yes.'

The line then plummets down to another diagonal, but a much steeper one this time.

'This is me,' Spencer's father says, jabbing at a low spot on the plummeting diagonal.

'OK,' Spencer says.

His father then continues the line another half-inch, punctuating its end with a vicious jab.

'And then it's goodbye Charlie.'

Spencer's father sits back again with his arms crossed like a classroom child who has been provoked out of his sullenness to teach his teacher a lesson.

'So there's no compensation? There's nothing good?'

'Shit. All shit,' Spencer's father says.

When Spencer was seventeen, he dropped out of school. He travelled around England, hitching lifts, staying with benevolent strangers and drinkers who befriended him in pubs and the families of people who knew people he knew in London. He spent his cash on fried breakfasts, beer and a haircut, and when he ran out of money he returned home. This was 1984. When Spencer's father was seventeen, it was 1939, the Germans were occupying Warsaw, and he left his city for the Soviet Union.

'Who was that guy who used to come around sometimes when we lived in New Jersey?'

'What guy?'

Spencer has a memory of a cheerfully mournful man sitting in the living room of their house in Berkeley Heights, nattily dressed, legs swinging because his father's armchair was a little too high for most visitors, looking tired and wretched behind his smile.

'A guy. You used to know him from the army or the camps or maybe back in Warsaw. He used to visit you a few times.'

'Visit me? Where?'

'In New Jersey. He was always very well dressed.'

'Oh yes! Zig Pianko.'

Spencer's father's pleasure is in his ability to recall the name rather than any emotion that the name or the memory of Zig Pianko evokes.

'He used to visit us. In New Jersey,' Spencer's father says.

'That's right,' Spencer says.

'He would sit there and I would sit there and we had not a thing to say to each other. It was heartbreaking.'

'Where did you know him from? From the War?'

'Yeah. The War.'

The difficulty of choosing an actor to play Spencer's father—film shoots drag on, extremities of cold and boredom, what actors are really paid for is to sit around doing nothing without making a fuss about it, which is not conducive to the well-being of the impatient and the frail; even the most generous insurance company might baulk at Spencer's father being hired to play himself—but the greatest difficulty would be to find someone who could do justice to his voice. Spencer's father's voice is a beautiful thing. It occupies a resonant low register, lower than Spencer's, and even though Spencer's father can't sing (and seems to take pleasure in the fact that his son is equally ill fitted for music and sports, as if Spencer's incapacities somehow validate his own), his speaking voice is baritone-musical, a joy for child Spencer to listen to on those rare occasions in his childhood when his father could be persuaded to tell his stories of Charlie and his two friends conducting their dangerous missions in wartime.

But it is Jimmy Ludwig's accent that makes his voice so special. Max von Sydow could possibly do it, or maybe Armin Mueller-Stahl. In Jimmy Ludwig's voice is a memory and a scar of every place he has ever lived. He thinks he speaks like an American, because when he moved from the Old World to the New, he believed, and continues to believe, that America is a place without class, where any foreigner can prove himself with diligence, where the holder of a US passport and a good credit rating is an American gentleman as fine as any with an Ivy League degree and money earned by a long-dead family member whose grubbiness has been smoothed away by time and a Boston accent, but to anyone's ear he speaks like a Polish-Russian-English-American. Here is pre-War Warsaw, there Siberia 1941, here's a trace of Italy 1944, here London 1946–51, and the Yankee overlay, his pronunciation of buoy as *boo-ee* and route as *rowt*, hides nothing.

'I knew him from then,' his father says.

Spencer supposes that the Poles don't have a *th* sound, because his father uses a *t* or a *d*. *I knew him from den,* or *Dat's terrific!* Or *'t ting is . . . In'credible!* In the gaps within the words, lost worlds appear. Spencer has a memory of his mother teasing his father in the living room of Berkeley Heights (one of those rare weekend occasions when his father wasn't working, or asleep on the sofa, or busying himself with illicit rendezvous—and who could blame him? He had been in Siberia, where he could not raise an erection to buy himself some extra food). In her almost impeccable English accent she was trying once again to teach him to perform the dental fricative: *Rest your tongue between your teeth and blow gently out around it . . . Go on, you do it, say, The teeth*, and his father said *T'e teet* and blew little bubbles of saliva around his words, which infant Spencer thought was sort of magical, because he was not above making those kinds of sounds and oral expulsions himself.

Zig Pianko gave up on making approaches to Spencer's father. His father had no time for the past. Spencer's father, if pressed about the past, would complain about the lack of love he received from his parents. *It's in'credible! I never had a birt'day party!* Spencer felt as if he were being blamed for it.

In a film of his father's life, maybe his father could play himself. Dress him in baggy trousers and school cap, put a bicycle chain in his hand and discreetly film from afar on a dangerous Warsaw street.

'Have you ever acted?'

After his father has been made to understand the question, he looks at Spencer as if he has been asked if he has recently been caught masturbating in public or knowingly bought a German product.

'How do you represent the past?'

The movie *Atlantic City*, which Spencer, ever the literalist, had watched before leaving London, is from a far-past time. In the opening scene, Susan Sarandon switches on a cassette player. In the second scene, there is a piece of business with a public payphone. People smoke in bars.

Tootie-Frootie ice cream and craps don't mix.

When Burt Lancaster tells Susan Sarandon that he watches her, window into window, adjoining apartments across the way, as she performs her post-oyster bar depiscinising routine of rubbing herself with lemon juice and perfume, she takes a moment to consider. And her response? She loosens her shirt and comes towards him. This is the sort of moment in films that Spencer despises.

When his father can be persuaded to turn his attentions away from the symptoms of his decline, they move into irritation at their slow progress behind the Academy bus and rest on his disappointments at his son. He doesn't say it, even a man so immune to tact as Jimmy Ludwig doesn't say it, but the question is there: I survived my youthful ordeals, my family died, for this? *This* is the summit of our civilisation? This is our culmination and consummation?

To his father's credit, he does not consider himself a special case. He is not ashamed to have survived, he never sought out the company of others with any kinds of similar experiences. He did not want to reminisce with Zig Pianko. He does not consider himself noble or heroic to be alive. He just wishes his son, in his status as the Last Man, were more worthy of the role.

'When are you going to get a job?'

'I have a job.'

Spencer can hear a whine in his voice, which he detests. His father is eighty-six years old, he is nearly forty-two, and Jimmy Ludwig still has the capacity to turn him into a child whose throat raws with self-pity as he tries to prove himself to his father.

'Your plays.'

'Yes. My films.'

On the occasions that Spencer's films have been shown in New York, his father has politely sat through screenings, at the Film Forum, the Kitchen, once at Lincoln Center, twice at the cinema that used to be in the basement of Carnegie Hall. His wife, Spencer's stepmother, used to come to them too, at the beginning, and she had attended the first of these events dressed according to her idea of a costume appropriate for a movie premiere, jewellery and furs. Neither of them has ever come to an after-screening party, for which Spencer is not ungrateful.

'It's your night,' his father had said the first time he had rejected the invitation. 'Enjoy.'

'It would be nice if you could be there,' Spencer had said entirely insincerely.

'Nice for who?' his father said.

Spencer's father was seldom forthcoming with his opinions of Spencer's films, and Spencer could never be sure which he was protecting, Spencer's standing in his landscape of imagined achievement and respect, or his own untutored uncertainty in a foreign world.

There are many things that Spencer is not sure of about his

father. How long the overlapping crossover period had been between his two wives, for example. But, the most fundamental and most unanswerable question Spencer has for his father (not a matter of dates, or the amount of money he has in the bank, or whether he had ever believed himself to be in love with his first wife, and when had he fallen out of love and life with his second wife and seen her, finally, for who she is; and indeed whether he believed in love; and why he had rejected most of the people he had ever been close to; and what was the origin of the feud his family had with their next-door neighbours when Spencer was young; and is his father aware of how many financial metaphors he uses to describe his transactions with people and the world; and what he thinks of his son, truly, is Spencer such a disappointment to him as it appears, or is there an amount of respect to be had for a man who made his way in a difficult world that Jimmy Ludwig could have no under-standing of?; and why he could have such an acute intelligence for systems and such an emptiness of response when it came to emotions, other people's), the question that occupies Spencer most of all while knowing that it can never be answered is whether the person his father is had been determined by his experiences in wartime, or whether the person he is is what had enabled him to survive.

Somewhere, less than a hundred miles from where they drift down the Parkway, is the ranch-style wooden house where Spencer spent the first six years of his life.

Their next-door neighbours were the Weathers family. Between the Ludwigs and the Weathers was some unspoken animosity that was never explained to Spencer, beyond that it was not permitted for him to go into their house nor to invite the two Weathers girls into his. The younger Weathers girl, who was just a few months older than Spencer, was called Mary-Lou. Mary-Lou Weathers had a fragilely pretty face and light brown corkscrew curls. She was fascinating to Spencer because of her shamelessly brazen habit of picking her nose in public and studiously eating what she retrieved. Once, fearful and thrilled, Spencer broke the rule against entry. He was with a group of neighbourhood kids on the Weathers' lawn. Mary-Lou invited the group in, not specifically excluding Spencer, but she knew as well as he did that he would not be able to come. Nonetheless, Spencer joined the group, waited for something enormous and biblical to occur as he walked slowly stutteringly in, trying to pretend he was a man of the world who often walked into his neighbours' houses, and stood at the edge of Mary-Lou's bedroom as she showed off her new Barbie doll.

Spencer was not especially interested in Barbie dolls but he was excited to be in the forbidden place. No one asked him what he was doing there. Nothing awful or even interesting happened to him in Mary-Lou Weathers's bedroom. After a few minutes, his bravery proved, his curiosity unappeased, he went back home again.

'So,' his father says.

'What?' Spencer says.

'When are you going to make a living?'

'I refuse to judge the value of what I do by how much money it makes.'

This would be edited straight out of the movie. Spencer's films have been accused of many things, but pomposity is not one of them. Not even the literary ones that used to be commissioned by the BBC, modernist journeys inspired by fragmentary heroes, Pessoa, Cortázar, Barrett. There are times he has tried to concentrate on plot but all that achieved was slowness. He has never possessed Rick Violet's single demonstrable skill, of moving characters quickly out of rooms. He has, he could remind his father, won prizes with his films. *Trudy Tuesday, History of the Tango, The Late George Reid, The Captain's Grief, Sonata for Piano and Violence, Robert W's Last Walk* have all been shown at international festivals and received awards. His most recent film, *Vertigo*, commissioned, but never shown, by Channel 4, was written about with some disquiet by those few critics who pay attention to Spencer Ludwig's career as if it was his most personal work, when anyone paying any kind of attention should have realised that it was, without question, his least.

His father does not shake his head. He does not even deign to raise an eyebrow.

'And I have a job, what you understand by job, at the film school.'

'Full-time?'

There are just a few topics where Jimmy Ludwig's language does not fail him. Most of them involve money.

'Well, no. Two days a week.'

This is not in fact true. It is, if Spencer were to be honest with himself, a lie. His teaching takes up at most one day a week.

'You make enough money?'

'Sort of. Up to a point.'

'The first responsibility of a man is to provide for her family.'

The pompous sententiousness of this is alleviated only slightly by his father's trouble with pronouns. Perhaps that is what this film should be called, *The Trouble with Pronouns*. Bitter-sweet and poignant, an old man's decline, the son as witness, memory the enemy.

'You remind me of the story,' Jimmy Ludwig says.

'What story?'

He wishes he hadn't asked. He has better things to do than play the role of his father's stooge.

'The fellow who shovelled shit in the circus. Well, he said, at least I'm in show business!'

Vengefully, Spencer twists the wheel, pulls out into the fast lane and speeds past the Academy bus. He is childishly pleased by the sight of his father hurled back into his seat.

'Tell me something,' Spencer says when they have each returned to some kind of equilibrium.

'What's that?'

'You remember the Weathers?'

'The what?'

'Our next-door neighbours when we lived in Berkeley Heights. The Weathers family. They lived next door to us. When I was a child, in New Jersey. The Weathers.'

'Sure I remember them. He was a moron.'

'You fell out with them. I wasn't allowed in their house. What was the fight?'

'I told you. He was a fuckin' moron.'

Spencer is pleased by the discovery that in contempt, even recollected contempt, his father's ability with pronouns improves. He is less pleased by the pursuing sound of a police siren. He slows, pulls into the right lane to let the police car cruise by. It does not pass him; the car, New Jersey State Trooper, settles in behind him, lights flashing red and blue. An automated voice orders him to pull over to the side of the road.

Spencer has never been stopped by the police before in the US. He has seen it often enough on television shows, witnessed it on New York City streets, men, usually dark skinned, sitting placid in their cars, policemen leaning in through the open driver's window, shining in a torch, the police car behind still flashing its lights. Light equals virtue and law and order. Darkness and blackness are the signifiers of lawless secrets and sins. He knows, in a learned observational way, that when a driver is stopped by the police in the United States he stays in his car. Nonetheless, when he pulls on to the hard shoulder of the Garden State Parkway, his father beside him saying, *What the . . .? What?*, after he puts the Cadillac into park, after the siren behind him has swirled into silence, he opens the driver's door.

And an amplified voice barks at him.

Stay where you are! Sir! Switch off your engine and stay in your car!

Poised, frozen, not sure how to follow the mixed instructions, Spencer stays where he is, one foot on the tarmac, one hand on the door handle, his bald patch naked and exposed.

'What are you doing now?' his father asks.

Sir! Get back into your car!

'You're an idiot,' his father says.

'Broke the mould, I know,' Spencer says.

And a force reaches him, not the crash upon his unprotected head that he had been unconsciously expecting, but a grip tight as metal on his arms, and he is pulled and lifted, shoved, delivered against the side of the car, the wheel arch cutting cruelly into his shins, his chest squeezed against the bonnet—or *hood*, he supposes he should call it—his head forced to one side so his view is the windshield, and the wipers that have been triggered in the commotion, and his father's face behind glass, a false-tooth smile, and a look that he is so unaccustomed to seeing that it takes him a while to register as pleasure.

'Please,' Spencer says.

The policeman's body pins him uncomfortably twisted between body and car. The breath of the policeman is hot on his face. Spencer detects the scent of burnt cheese and engine oil and beer. He wonders if this is what it feels like to be in one of those underground sex clubs with names like Anvil and Hoist.

'I'm sorry,' Spencer says.

The policeman pulls Spencer's wrists hard together. A knee rams into the small of his back. Spencer grunts in pain.

'I'm English,' Spencer says.

Through the windscreen, his father's expression moves from pleasured to troubled. At first Spencer is grateful for his concern, then is reminded of the panicky expression his father's face shows when he is in some urgency of urinating.

'My father,' Spencer says.

And the policeman breathes harder, holds him tighter. Spencer will never know whether it's the decrepitude of his father or his own nationality that has protected him, but the policeman has relented, and he is no longer being squeezed to the side of the car. He may even wiggle his wrists a little inside the policeman's grip. The most alarming thing is that his father seems to be having a fit or a seizure of some kind. The right side of his face clenches, twists and drops. It is like an awful parody of a wink. It might, Spencer considers, Spencer hopes, actually be a wink.

'Get back into your car, sir,' the policeman says, not unkindly, almost, it might be said, fatherly.

'Yes. Thank you.'

Spencer scuttles back into the driver's seat and scrupulously rests his arms on the steering wheel to show the policeman that not only does he mean no harm but that he would be incapable of providing it.

'Thank you,' Spencer says.

'I'd like to see your driving licence, sir,' the policeman says.

'A leak,' Spencer's father says.

'Um. Please. My father? He has a very small and irritable bladder.'

For the first time Spencer and the policeman look at each other face to face. The policeman is older than Spencer had expected and is proud and careworn. He also looks as if he suspects Spencer of making fun of him.

'I need a leak,' his father says.

'Oh. OK. We can do that,' the policeman says.

Spencer sets about getting out of the car but the policeman pushes him back down again.

'Stay where you are, sir, and leave your arms where I can see them.'

Spencer feels that this is a little unfair, as he has his arms in plain view, and he is troubled at the prospect of retrieving his wallet from his back pocket in order to show the policeman his driving licence while keeping his arms still.

'I was going to help my father.'

'We'll take care of it, sir.'

His father is looking less panicky, almost smug. The policeman speaks into his walkie-talkie and soon they are joined by a second policeman, who opens the front passenger door, and courteously, solicitously, eases Spencer's father out of the car and to the edge of the hard shoulder. Discreetly, he stands with his back to Spencer's father and holds his jacket out wide to shield the undraped man from the view of other motorists.

'Your licence, sir. Slowly, sir.'

Spencer eases forward to reach into the back pocket of his jeans and pull out his wallet. He finds his driver's licence and presents it to the policeman, whose name is Porrelli.

'I'm English, this is an English licence,' Spencer says.

'So I see.'

'Look. I'm sorry. I'm really sorry. What's the problem? Was I speeding? I don't think I was speeding, I'm used to English roads where the speed limits are higher. I—'

'This is not about speeding, sir.'

'Oh. Good. I mean. Oh. Then. Oh, I get it. Littering. It's the business with the phones isn't it? Some highway ordinance, I'm sure. I told my father—'

The other policeman escorts Spencer's father back to the car.

'You see?! I told you something would happen,' Spencer says.

'No one likes a whiner,' Spencer's father says.

'I'm sorry,' Spencer says. 'I told him not to, I said we'd get into trouble. I should have gone back and looked for them, but he needed to make a . . . a rest stop, you know, men's room, comfort station, he has a small and irritable bladder, and I didn't think we had the time, so I'm very sorry. Is there a fine for this sort of thing?'

'She's always been a whiner,' Spencer's father says. 'When she was a baby she used to bang her head.'

'Sir, does your father have any ID?'

'Dad? Could you show this gentleman some ID?'

'Absolutely.'

His father does not move.

'Dad. Your wallet.'

'What about it?'

'Can I have it for a moment?'

'What is this? They want money?'

'He, this gentleman, the police officer, just wants to see some ID.'

'Forget about it. They're not getting a nickel.'

His father crosses his arms stubbornly across his chest.

Wildly, Spencer considers tickling his father. Before his neuropathy set in, he had always been very ticklish.

'Sir. We need to see your father's ID.'

'Yes yes, I know.'

If this were an independent film, what would happen? They would end up as best friends, just for one night, the four of them in a roadside bar drinking beer and discovering astonishing synchronicities; or it would turn into torture and labyrinth, the hint of unspeakable horrors in a rural cellar where no light shines and nothing is real except for the imminence of pain and execution. If it were one of Spencer's films, then not much would happen, he has to admit. The day would pass, night would fall, morning might break upon this frozen tableau.

'Not a red nickel,' his father says.

If this were one of Rick's films, if this were one of Rick's *early* films, a shoot-out would probably ensue, or a song, bright colour pastiche, stolen emotion and borrowed resonance. Spencer has never received the credit that he had avoided taking for Rick's early successes. He had scripted them and shot them and done it all with a freedom that was unavailable to him for work he produced under his own name. If this were one of Rick's, as the fawning critics like to say, *mature* works, what would happen? Something casual and opaque that hinted at philosophical depths because Rick did not have the intellect or the technique to reach into them directly. He could only imply and hope, no, *know*, that the critics and the audiences would pander to his engorged sense of his own capacities.

'Sir,' says Officer Porrelli.

'What's going to happen? Is there a fine or something?'

'Sir?'

'Littering, I suppose it would be. He threw it out of the window, and I—'

And Spencer feels guilty. Why should he give up his father in this way? Was this going to be the start of something?— anything that goes wrong in his life, he would blame his father because his father was sick and vulnerable and couldn't look after himself.

'He threw what out of the window, sir?'

'This isn't because of that?'

'Of what?'

'You haven't said sir.'

'Excuse me?'

'Sir. I'm sorry. It's just that I'd got used to you saying sir in every sentence.'

The look in Porrelli's eye is the one that he had had before, when it was accompanied by grip and restraint and barroom pizza-parlour breath and the threat of the bad things that policemen are entitled to do to fathers and sons who have put themselves in opposition to the law.

Long ago, when he was in his father's company, in Long Island summers on his father's boat, or at meals where gruffly self-made men would display their chests and their women and pretend to be humorous by pausing with silver carving knife to brusquely interrogate the other males at the table whether they were leg or breast men, Spencer had felt any part of himself that had the potential for power or extension in the world become small and timid, looking for, expecting, protection from his father's strength. As a child, Spencer had always made the mistake of confusing self-assurance with knowledge. Ever since his father first became sick, Spencer had grown into some kind of adulthood. He could not trust his father's strength. And his father's self-assurance could be most vehement when it was most obviously wrong.

Spencer has given up any thought of help from his father, so he is surprised when his father reaches for his wallet and with scrabbling neuropathic fingers manages to prise out his driving licence and pass it to Spencer.

'Give this to the gentleman,' his father says.

Porrelli compares his father's driving licence to Spencer's. He steps away from the car and lowers his chin to speak into his walkie-talkie.

'It's her,' his father says.

'Who?'

'Your mother,' his father says.

Spencer's mother died years before, surprised by death similarly to how she had been disappointed by life. For a moment, he struggles with the notion that his father has been granted something additional and perhaps compensatory, that he is drifting into the shade between this world and the next, which means, contrary to all Spencer's knowledge and intuition, that there is an afterlife, and that his father, in some kind of senescently sentimental dance, is back in step with his lost, dead, under-loved first wife.

'She called them. Your mother.'

And he realises that it is his stepmother that his father must be referring to. And indeed, when Porrelli returns to the car, he tells them that his father had been reported by his wife as a missing person.

'He's not missing. He's with me,' Spencer says.

'Your mother reported him as missing. *Sir.*'

'She's not my mother. She's my stepmother.'

'You might want to make a call to your mother.'

'I would. If I—'

And his father looks at Spencer and looks at Porrelli and in an effort of recollection, of recohesion that makes Spencer wonder how much psychic and physical energy it will have cost him, says,

'I am taking a drive with my son. My wife is crazy. Frankly her credibility with me right now is zero. No one should listen to her. I am sure you have many important duties to to to. To do to.'

It is a courtroom speech, a summing-up to convince judge and jury and witnesses. Apart from its stuttering conclusion, it is a masterly performance. Porrelli hands back the licences—to Spencer's father rather than to Spencer.

'Have a good day sir,' Porrelli says.

'Thank you,' Spencer says.

'Enjoy New Jersey.'

'Goodbye Charlie,' Spencer's father says. 'Let's move it.'

After their escape from the New Jersey troopers, the mood is lighter, easier, this is something father and son have done together, think what they could do now, a murder spree, a daring bank job, get jobs as ferrymen on a lonely river, discover philosophy and wildlife in the tranquil rhythms of their trade—and the film that they could be making, Danny DeVito as Spencer, Walter Matthau as Jimmy, except DeVito is too old and Matthau is dead. Fantasy casting is an easy game to play—Kirk and Michael Douglas, Henry and Peter Fonda, Lee J. Cobb and Frank Sinatra—but this one could be real.

'You remember Lee J. Cobb?'

'Who?'

'Lee J. Cobb, the actor. *On the Waterfront*, remember?—Johnny Friendly, the union boss. Big guy, sort of brooding and scary. Always intimidated me. Reminded me of you, to be honest. Lee J. Cobb.'

'Lee Cobb,' his father says, and the gap between words and their meaning is so wide that chasms open up in the car that the world and its weather fall into. Leaving Jimmy Ludwig alone and cold with his back pain and his bladder condition and his constipation, and Spencer has ruined the mood.

'Lee J. Cobb,' Spencer insists.

And something happens. Words to ear, an internal percussion drums into the cochlea, electricity pulses, neurons spark, synapses connect to dendrites and axons of neighbouring cells, and somehow, in Jimmy Ludwig's brain, there are still enough willing neurotransmitters to ferry the electricity across the synaptic gaps, and the name Lee J. Cobb continues on its difficult route, detouring around the cells that died in 2001 when Jimmy Ludwig suffered his stroke, and memory comes alight. In some dingy place of his recollection, a movie star's face and manner and name are suddenly apparent and accessible, and this is one of the miracles of film.

'Yes! Sure! Lee J. Cobb!' Spencer's father says, and his ensuing smile is open and broad and he rests a wavery hand on Spencer's arm in gratitude.

'His real name was Leo Jacoby,' Spencer says, regretting this instantly, concerned that the extra information will open up the chasm again.

'That's terrific,' his father says. 'My name used to be Izio.'

'I know,' Spencer says. 'The teeth.'

'What's that?' (*What's dat?*)

'The teeth.'

'Yes,' Spencer's father says. '*T'e teet.*'

Spencer's tired heart is filled with love, and the road slides down to the ocean.

Chapter Four

'What are we?' Spencer's father asks, meaning where.

'Atlantic City, always turned on,' Spencer says.

The skyline is hardly Las Vegas, and it's hardly Louis Malle either, the casino resorts stubbing out into the greyness of the ocean sky, but Spencer feels the familiar lift of excitement that he always has whenever he reaches a place dedicated to gambling. He never expects to feel it, which is maybe why it is so reliable.

'We're looking for a place called the Horseshoe. Keep your eyes peeled.'

'What is this? Vegas?' his father says.

'Atlantic City,' Spencer says.

'A dump,' his father says.

Already Spencer feels protective towards the town. If any place tries this hard to make something happen, even if it is only its own profiteering, then he thinks it should be given a chance.

Tropicana, Taj Mahal, Caesar's Palace, Golden Lion, Ballys,

Wild West, the road pulls away from the ocean, which they can still smell, its salty tang of seawater and waste, the billboards assert this is a place for fun, welcoming not gamblers but *gamers*, they drive past an empty street of high-end boutiques that looks like a set from a zombie movie, the capitalist system dead, the world void of consumers, and all there will be left is unwanted products and hollow people, the theory of surplus anti-value, and there is the Horseshoe, concrete and shimmer, a hermaphrodite of a building with its five-storey ring surrounding a high tower. They follow the sign to valet parking, and a man older than Spencer in orange shorts and jacket runs to the El Dorado to open Spencer's father's door.

Jimmy Ludwig grunts and twists and succeeds, on his third attempt, in heaving himself out of the car. The valet offers an experienced arm, which he ignores, preferring to rest his diminishing weight on the hood of the car. Spencer gathers up their belongings, the backpack and backgammon set, his father's cane, the baggies with provisions, and manages, adroitly, he is getting better at this, to exchange a dollar bill for a ticket stub from the valet and sweep up the oxygen cylinder before his father tugs it cataclysmically along behind him, and give his father his shoulder to lean on for the short walk to the Horseshoe entrance, all without breaking stride or sweat or wind.

The lobby desk is an optimistically long counter to which red velvet ropes mark out different lines for silver, gold and platinum customers. The only queue is the one for silver guests, at which a huddle of old people wait bovine while the desk clerk deals with a gold couple who seem set on questioning every aspect of their accommodation.

'Ocean view,' says the man.

'You have an ocean view,' the clerk says.

'Not from the bathroom,' the woman says with the manner of an expert negotiator accustomed to clinching every transaction, financial or personal, to the detriment of her opponent, a way of being that Spencer is familiar with in his stepmother.

He is wondering whether he might just push into the platinum line where an unoccupied clerk gazes forlornly out, when he and his father are approached by two people, one male, one female, similarly rotund and black haired and small, and dressed identically in black Converse sneakers and black jeans and black T-shirts that have a white-line drawing of the Atlantic City Boardwalk and the legend *Short Beach Film Festival 2008* across their lumpy breasts. They each carry clipboards and film festival plastic bags.

Spencer is gratified until they both walk past him to take hold of his father. One tries to kiss him, the other grabs his hand to pull it up and down.

'Sir,' says the male.

'An honour,' says the female.

Slightly panicked, Spencer's father retracts the pieces of his body that had been occupied and looks to Spencer for assistance.

'Dwight?' says the male.

The overworked desk clerk elegantly raises an eyebrow and smiles with a glint of white and gold.

'Will you look after these gentlemen? Your best possible care.'

'Of course,' Dwight the desk clerk says with an impressive implication that he would consider it a spiritual failing to intend any less.

'This is your itinerary,' the male says.

'And your goody bag!' the female says.

'I . . .' says Spencer.

But he is hushed with a brisk dismissive handshake from the male and a present of a goody bag from the female.

'Mike and Cheryl are devastated,' says the female.

'That's Mr Baumbach and Mrs Baumbach. The festival organisers.'

'Devastated that they can't be here to greet you in person.'

'They are so looking forward to meeting you.'

'Gala.'

'On Friday.'

'You'll be at the top table.'

'Of course he will. That goes without saying.'

'I was just letting him *know*,' the male says, somewhat petu-lantly.

Inside the bag is a guidebook to Atlantic City, two pens with the Short Beach Film Festival logo and the same T-shirt these two reps are wearing. Spencer likes black T-shirts. He will wear just about any slogan and condition of black T-shirt.

'Have you come direct from Tirana?' the male asks.

'Absolutely,' Spencer's father says.

'You must be tired after your trip.'

'Sure, absolutely.'

'I can't say—'

'*We.*'

'We can't say what an honour this is.'

'Wow. Just. Wow.'

'We'd like to show you the press pack we have.'

And Spencer is jealous of the attention that his father is getting which is meant to be his. He hadn't known quite what he was expecting from their arrival, but it certainly isn't this, to be standing unregarded with oxgyen tanks and rucksack and backgammon set. His father has even eaten the Milano biscuits that his step-mother had packed for him.

'I'm Spencer Ludwig,' Spencer says.

'Are you his interpreter?'

'In a manner of speaking.'

'He speaks very good English, doesn't he?'

'Up to a point. But look—'

'What did you say your name was?'

'Is. Is. Ludwig. Spencer Ludwig.'

'That's a coincidence.'

'Really? What is?'

'One of our guests has that name. He's a director too.'

'I think that'll probably be me.'

'Well that is a coincidence, isn't it? We had no idea. Dwight?'

The festival reps visit the desk and talk to the clerk.

'Who are these jokers?' Spencer's father says.

'They seem to think you're somebody important. How's your Albanian?'

After the reps have flurried away, Spencer receives room keys from the desk clerk. Looking at his father leaning with difficulty on the desk, Spencer asks if a wheelchair might be available.

'Not a problem, sir. I shall procure you a wheelchair.'

'I'm very grateful.'

'Not at all. It's what we do. We're here to expedite and facilitate your felicitude.'

The desk clerk tries not to show his pride in his own vocabulary. He speaks in an almost offhand way as if there is nothing to remark upon in his choice of words. The pride shows through nonetheless.

'Oh. Great. Thanks.'

The desk clerk is in his early twenties. He will, Spencer suspects, go far.

'Thank you Dwight.'

'You're most welcome. And I believe there's a message for you, Mister Ludwig, from a British gentlewoman named Michelle.'

Spencer accepts the slip of paper and crumples it unread into a pocket of his jeans, and Dwight disappears and reappears pushing a heavy metal wheelchair with the words Property of Atlantic City Medical Center Do Not Remove painted across its backrest.

'Oh. Great. Thanks. And, uh, Dwight?'

'Sir?'

'One other thing?'

'Of course. Yours to name and mine to satisfy or rectify.'

'This might be a more difficult one to arrange. But we're running low on oxygen. I don't know if you can tell us where, how, we might facilitate . . .?'

'You require a refill or some new tanks or both? We can expedite *and* facilitate. Leave it with me, sir.'

By the time that Spencer has navigated his grumbling father to subside into the wheelchair and laid his cane across his twitching lap (his legs inside his flapping trousers seem even skinnier than when they had set out on this journey), and hung their carrier bags from the wheelchair handles and manoeuvred his father (so light, so dry) up the ramp out of the reception area, and through the colonies of slot machines, and into the elevator (backwards was, he thought, easier and more considerate but, he discovers, if he turns his father to the wall, removes any stimulus from him, then he becomes less troublesome and prickly) and along the brown corridor to their room, and opens the door, there is already a suite of oxygen equipment installed.

'I'll have to give Dwight a good tip,' Spencer says.

His father looks doubtfully at the room.

'It's a shithole,' he says.

'Which bed do you want?'

This is all getting more intimate than Spencer had anticipated. In his projection of their arrival, he had imagined gaming tables and showgirls, the respect paid to his work and career; he had not thought about the arrangements of sleep and toilet, he had not pictured the damp patch spreading across his father's groin.

His father, to Spencer's slight alarm, removes his trousers and hangs them, with some fastidiousness, over the back of the chair that faces the vanity mirror. He yanks off his surgical collar and tosses it on to a bed. He then approaches Spencer, while pulling ineffectually at his shirt.

Spencer blinks. He can feel his lips involuntarily pursing in preparation for a kiss.

'My poppers,' Spencer's father says.

'Excuse me?'

'Poppers!'

Spencer's father waves his hands towards his shirt front.

'Your buttons?'

'What I said! Poppers!'

Spencer hurriedly unbuttons his father's shirt while his father averts his attention. This process cheers neither of them. Spencer hangs the shirt over the bedstead. He then sets about invalid-proofing the room. He drapes towels over the sharp edges of the furniture, rolls up the bathroom rug so his father won't snag his stick or his foot on it and fall on one of his innumerable night-time trips to the john; he pushes the wooden chair in tight to the dressing table; he situates the companion armchairs in the bay by the window so father and son can play backgammon more congenially.

His father is comfortable now. He sits on an armchair in his white briefs and black socks. Unlike Spencer he has hardly any hair on his body. And unlike Spencer he is skinny. Apart from one period in his early fifties, after he gave up smoking and developed a little pot belly that offended his vanity and which he banished in a few months with a careful diet, denying himself sugar and fats, while compensating by rewarding himself with even more salt, Spencer's father had always been thin and wiry-strong; Spencer had always tended to fat. And in his decline, his father has lost weight and bulk. Even his hands have lost their muscle tone. Spencer imagines lifting him, carrying him fretful around the room, cradling him and cooing to him.

'Here,' his father says.

He holds out his left arm, where his gold watch hangs around his wrist. If his decline were to be measured in time then his watch would be its most reliable recorder. Except the record would not be in hours, but in the gold links of the bracelet. Every month, every few weeks, another link would need to be removed to accommodate its owner's shrinking wrist.

'Can you?' Spencer's father says, shaking his arm.

'The watch? You want me to help you take it off?'

As he used to do when he was a child trying to concentrate, and maybe to offer his father a moment to return to his former tyrannical and entirely unhelpless state, Spencer's tongue protrudes between his lips as he battles to unclasp the watch from his father, who fails to respond to the bait.

'It's heavy,' Spencer says, weighing it in his hand.

'Eighteen-carat. Patek Philippe. It's yours.'

'Oh. No. Thank you.'

'You don't want it?'

Of course Spencer doesn't want it. The watch is an item of jewellery rather than a timepiece. It is clunky and gold and flashy, designed to suit a man who is flamboyantly sure of his sexuality or else deeply unsure. It corresponds to everything that Spencer's mother and Spencer too, loyally but not unthinkingly, had ever rejected in his father's attitude to life; and even if it accorded in any degree to Spencer's sense of style, which is founded, of course, on the movies, French café types in black and white waiting for Jean Gabin to show or Michèle Morgan to sing, William Powell mixing a highball, Robert Mitchum in a lounge suit, pushed out of his laziness to prove his strength, again—even though the only model he has ever come close to exemplifying is Jack Nicholson in *Easy Rider*—he still wouldn't want it.

Spencer doesn't wear watches. He has a combative, rebellious attitude towards the very notion of time. But there is something soft, close to pleading in his father's voice, which it would be rude, perhaps unloving, not to respond to.

'All right. Yes. Thank you. It's very . . . beautiful.'

Spencer, somewhat laboriously, fixes the watch to his own, much plumper wrist, which his father at least has the grace not to draw attention to. Spencer's father disapproves of fat, just as he disapproves of ugliness. Both are markers of negative moral equity.

'Have fun with it,' his father says. 'Now let's get to work.'

He subsides in the armchair, resting his elbows and naked arms at the round table beneath the window, which offers a rejected view of a clear grey sky.

Jimmy Ludwig's appetite for backgammon is insatiable. Spencer's only respite is when his father's questionable bladder demands frequent visits to the bathroom, which he makes totteringly, eschewing the cane, patting or grabbing at each hard surface he passes to help him on his way.

Spencer takes one of his father's bathroom breaks as the opportunity to call his stepmother. It is only right, he supposes, to let her know where her husband is.

'Hi, it's Spencer,' he unnecessarily says.

'I'll call you back. I'm waiting for the police. Your father. He still hasn't returned from Dr Gribitz. Do you have any idea—'

'He's with me, still with me. He's fine. We're fine.'

'What?!'

'We, uh, took a little drive.'

'Where *are* you?'

'Atlantic City.' (And how he doubts the words will contain any of the blistered ironic romance they still have for him.)

'*What??!*'

'Atlantic City.'

'Excuse me, Spencer. I heard you the first time. What the hell are you doing in Atlantic City?'

'I think I told you. There's a film festival here at which I'm a guest. They're showing a retrospective of my films—'

'Spencer. I do not, I am not . . .'

(New Yorkers clip their Ts so smartly, and he always experiences a little thrill, close to erotic, at the way New Yorkers pronounce words with two consecutive Ts in them, such as *battle*.)

'We're playing backgammon. He seems on very good form. I think the trip is good for him.'

'*What?* Where is he?'

'He's in the bathroom right now. He's fine.'

'Do you know how long it's been since he went anywhere?'

'No. How long?'

'That's not really the point is it? How long.'

'Well look. I just wanted to let you know. We'll be back in a couple of days. I'll deliver him safe and sound.'

'Do you *know* what you're doing, Spencer?'

(And he is reminded here of Rick Violet: his stepmother and Rick are the only people he knows who relentlessly use the name of the person they are talking to in conversation. His stepmother uses it as an attack weapon, Rick as an act of charm, but charm too is an aggressive act. He wonders if that is why he has an antipathy to each of them, and if so, which of them is the one who reminds him of the other. He has known his stepmother for longer, but it was only when he became friends with Rick that he realised just how much he disliked her.)

'Yes. Of course. I—'

'You're *killing him* is what you're doing.'

'Well no. I don't think so. We're fine. Really. Look. I'll get him to give you a call later after he gets out of the bathroom.'

'Please. Please do not bother yourself on my account. You just get on with killing your father and tell me when the funeral is. And are you going to call the police now? Are you the one who's going to tell them they've been wasting their time? Are you going to have to apologise?'

'Look. I—'

'And by the way, *Spencer*, where is my fucking toaster-oven?'

Spencer hangs up the phone, one beat ahead of his stepmother.

When his father returns from the bathroom, his face is beatific.

'I had a shit,' he proudly reports. 'My first in a month.'

Spencer had hoped for comradeship, maybe even an exchange of secrets. He would tell his father his artistic manifesto, and maybe in the telling discover for himself what it is. And his father would tell him stories of his childhood and youth and War years, first loves, dangerous travels, the Captain's griefs, and maybe, for once, tell him something about his first marriage, with Spencer's mother, that isn't designed to protect either Spencer's opinions or his own. They clack their pieces around the board and Spencer tries to initiate the frank exchange, but his father isn't having any of it.

'Tell me about your first marriage,' Spencer says, and his father pretends to hear this as an announcement by his son of an impending wedding.

'When's the happy day?' he says.

'Good question,' Spencer says.

'Make your mind up. You're not getting any younger.'

'Happy day,' Spencer says.

'I need a six and a one.'

When his father plays backgammon, his senses and concentration are attuned. He makes fewer aphasic mistakes with his language.

'You must have been happy once. When you were first married. An adventure. There must have been some love there.'

'Your turn,' his father says.

'Let's take a break,' Spencer says.

They have been playing for a couple of hours and he is hungry and tired and bored. But his father is on a winning streak (exploiting Spencer's hunger and tiredness and boredom) and never likes to quit when he is ahead.

'You had enough?' his father says, and Spencer is sufficiently competitive and ungenerous himself not to be able to relent.

They play on, until Spencer is dazed and irritable and seeing double. When he wins three boards on the trot, the final one by a gammon (*Incredible!* his father says, a less-used variant of *Disgusting!*), moving the score in his feverish favour to plus twenty-seven, which equates, at twenty-five cents a point, to a profit of $6.75, his father pushes peevishly at the table.

'OK. Don't play if your heart is not in it.'

Unkindly, Spencer says,

'No, it's OK, I'm getting my second wind now, we can play on.'

'No. You've had enough. You're tired. You've got a big day tomorrow.'

Spencer is touched that his father remembers that he has any kind of day coming up tomorrow. His tone is gruff but not unfatherly. And, on some level, which almost flatters Spencer, his father sees him as an aspect of himself, or at least finds a use for him as a way of declaring his own weakness without loss of face. Spencer relents.

'Yes. You're right. Jet lag. Maybe we should get something to eat. You hungry?'

His father purses his lips and shakes his head. His father never admits to such human weaknesses as hunger or tiredness or need.

'Well keep me company at any rate. We could go downstairs to eat or order something in.'

'Whichever you want. I'm not sleepy.'

On the third floor of the Horseshoe hotel-casino and resort are the conference rooms, where the festival is going to be. On the second floor are the bars and cafés and restaurants. Father and son sit at a round table in an Italian restaurant and Spencer looks at the few other occupied tables to see whether he can spot any other likely festival attendees, and his father looks at the menu as if he understands what he is seeing.

Spencer is pierced by guilt. This has been a most arduous day. His father customarily takes one walk a day into the hallway of the apartment, stands trying to be motionless by the elevator bank, while teetering and tottering because his body refuses to be still, conducting its treacheries and rebellions in the useless twitches of random nerve endings, the twists and gasps of dying muscle.

'I don't think we're ready to order yet,' Spencer says to the waiter who comes over to serve them.

'I'll have the . . .' his father says.

The waiter waits, puzzled.

'Cappuccino,' his father says.

'OK.'

'And a salad.'

'What sort of dressing would you like with that?'

'Calamari,' Spencer says.

'OK. But I just need to know what dressing the gentleman would like with his salad.'

'Calamari. He doesn't want cappuccino.'

'Oh. OK. And the dressing?'

'What dressing do you want?'

His father has already shut his menu and is looking around for the ice that a busboy had been ordered to bring.

'Dad? What dressing do you want on your salad?'

His father focuses on him.

'Medium rare.'

'He might want a steak.'

'Yeah. Steak. Medium rare.'

'OK. I have him for a cappuccino and calamari and salad and steak, medium rare. We'll get on in a moment as to whether he would like T-bone, porterhouse, sirloin or filet, brisket, New York, minute or chump. But what dressing would he care for on the salad?'

And oh it goes on, as it has gone on with the busboy and

the cocktail waitress and the maître d', as it will go on with everyone who demands something of Jimmy Ludwig, any stranger with a list of possibilities, anyone asking him to choose a noun that corresponds to an intimation of desire. His father expresses little desire because it is such a struggle to find words to signify any. Or his father experiences no desire and his vocabulary has etiolated accordingly, words dropping away from his control along with all the rest.

Spencer practises a funeral encomium at their casino restaurant table. At first he says it in his head but the silence has grown hateful. He had pushed his father's wheelchair past the International Buffet, which had been at least busy, obese diners in electric wheelchairs whizzing from table to counter from one cuisine to another, Italian, South-East Asian, Southern Fried, and skeletal diners sitting alone, so slowly lifting fork to mouth. And none of them looked like New Jersey or Albanian filmmakers, just gamblers down on their luck. Here, at Lucio's, Spencer and his father are almost alone, their silence broken by the occasional clatter when the kitchen doors swing open, the clink of fresh ice brought by the busboy.

'My father,' Spencer says, 'could not be described as having a genius for friendship. If ever he could be persuaded to visit somebody else's house, it wouldn't take long for him to look at his watch, make some kind of an attempt at a rueful smile, and say, *Well, it's been nice*, and get up to leave . . . No. It's probably bad to begin with a negative, isn't it? Even though it might be in keeping. My father was the toughest and in some ways the smartest man I ever met.'

The subject of the speech, who had naughtily been allowed to leave the surgical collar in the room, has his chin tight to his chest, as he saws at the piece of meat that he has not permitted Spencer to cut up for him.

'A lot of you here will already know some of my father's history.'

Spencer looks around the restaurant as if he were surveying the mourners in a funeral chapel. But who would be here? His stepmother, of course, and Jacksie and his wife Ellie, and his other stepbrother, who performs shady transactions in poorer parts of the developing world. His stepmother's cousin and her husband, if they were able to make the journey, because the latest word from them was that her cancer was getting worse and the quantities of steroid he was taking for his pulmonary condition were sending him amok, berserk. Maybe their daughter, Spencer's step-cousin, if she was out of rehab again. His stepmother's lawyer. His father's accountant and his father's broker. A representative from the building, either James the elevator operator or Philippe the doorman. Anybody else? He did not think he would take Mary to Papa Jimmy's funeral. Who would he be orating to? He would be speaking his father's life to air and to people who didn't know whether to exult or grieve that they had outlasted Jimmy Ludwig.

'My father was born in Warsaw in 1922. His family was middle-class in a sort of undistinguished way. Does this matter? Do your class origins matter? I suppose they do. How's the steak? He was a rebellious boy, expelled, I think, from six different schools. When he was seventeen, the Germans occupied Poland. It was not a good time to be a Jew in Warsaw. It was going to get worse, unimaginably so, but all the same, if you could get out, it was wise to do so. So my father and a friend of his, who was called Benny, went east, to Białystok, which was being occupied by the Soviets.'

The audience would be staring at Spencer with a mixture of indifference and dislike. He would want to do justice to his father. The meaning of a life is not provided by its end. He would say that.

'The meaning of a life is not provided by its end. My father's last years were not happy. He was a vigorous man, who despised his own failings. It was horribly frustrating and galling to him to be handicapped in the ways he was. When he had his stroke that was the first time he was ever in a hospital. No, I better not, no thank you.'

The waiter takes away his empty martini glass.

'His history was extraordinary. That isn't quite right. His history was extraordinary to most of those he would come into contact with later on in life. But it was an ordinary one for his place and time. The extraordinary thing was that he survived it. One aunt and one uncle of his also survived being a Jew in Warsaw in 1939. We had him in Białystok. Seventeen years old. Boy rebel, teenage communist. Of course he should be in the Soviet Union. Except the Soviet Union isn't so good. He gets a job in a magnesium factory in Kaminsk. He loses the job in the magnesium factory in Kaminsk. He's in the Ural mountains now, one of thousands of displaced Polish nationals trying to make it through a Russian winter. So, he decided to head back west. He made it as far as a town called Kowno, where, the story as my father tells it, told it, there was word put out that any Pole wanting a free train ride back to Warsaw should gather at the station at a certain time. No one there knew what was going on back home, but it had to be better than this. So two thousand people cram into cattle trucks, but after a day or so they realised they were going the wrong way. They end up in Siberia, in a forced labour camp, laying railway tracks.'

How much detail should he go into? That they had to build their own shelter for that first winter? That his father would pretend to faint once a month so he could spend a couple of days in the hospital shack?

But he's got the order wrong. There's the episode in Moscow to tell them about, and that comes first, the May Day celebrations. It is one of his favourite episodes from his father's life, perhaps because nothing really happens in it. But he would have to go on, further into his description of camp life, hope that the pause would be interpreted as a manful struggle against excessive display of emotion.

'In the camps, they were given a basic ration of food, but there was an incentive to work for more. And productivity was measured by the amount of earth they had dug up and transported by cart. Most of the inmates of course were working themselves to death, because the extra rations couldn't compensate for the amount of energy they were expending; but none of them, these tough factory workers and farm hands, wanted my father in their work gangs, because he was too young and too scrawny and too Jewish. My father fell in with a gang of chancers and wasters, who would find other people's earth to claim as their own without having to transport it the extra couple of kilometres. So the burly Poles were dropping like flies and my father kept making it through.'

And should he retell the story that his father had once told him? About the women's camp, and the inmates' enticements? This probably wouldn't be an appropriate anecdote for the funeral oration. Except it was probably a significant experience for Jimmy Ludwig, the wrong lesson that was learned for later life. His father has always been a passionate man. Spencer has never thought of him as a sensual one.

'As I said, I think I said, he beat the odds on so many occasions. About six hundred survived of those two thousand who made the original journey to Siberia. (And meanwhile any Jews left in Białystok were wiped out after the Nazis occupied it. And we know what happened in Warsaw!) When the Germans broke the Molotov–von Ribbentrop pact, the Polish nationals, or what was left of them, were released from the camps. He had been there for sixteen months. He was given a loaf of bread, a kilo of herring, a jar of vegetables and the opportunity to join the Red Army. Instead he found his way south to where General Anders was forming a battalion of Poles that would later become part of the British Eighth Army. They marched, raggle-taggle and sick and malnourished, out of the USSR, made some kind of recuperation in Iran, where my father lay down, expecting to die.

'He didn't die. He didn't die then, in Iran or Iraq or Palestine. And he didn't die at the Battle of Monte Cassino, where he fired big guns in support of the assault. He ended up in London after the War, he survived all these things, and in London he was treated, he said, as a dirty foreigner. But he met his wife there, my mother, and they moved to America because that was a place where if you were smart and worked hard then you would be rewarded regardless of your origins. And it worked for him. He made money. He lost one wife, but he gained another, and for the first half of his second marriage at least, he was probably happier than he had ever been.

'I don't know whether he was fundamentally changed by his experiences, or being the person he was was what enabled him to survive them. That, and luck of course. He didn't talk about any of this until he was well into his seventies. He said he didn't see the point. He didn't seek out the company of anyone with similar experiences, and he didn't see the point of talking about something to someone who couldn't have the slightest idea of what he was talking about. Is there a Zig Pianko here? No. I didn't think so.

'He knew that surviving the things that happen to you doesn't make you into a hero.

'He wasn't a hero. He was selfish and obsessed by money, and didn't have any insight or even much interest in the inner lives of others. His primary methods of communication were interrogation and flirtation, and were he not my father I probably wouldn't have held any of that against him.'

Spencer's father has fallen asleep.

'I'm going to have to try this again. I don't think I quite hit the right note,' Spencer says.

Chapter Five

Spencer has no memory of ever sharing a bedroom with his father before. He once took a shower with his father and was disappointed to see that his father's penis was smaller than he would have expected. *Runs in the family*, Spencer's father had said, before commenting on the hair on Spencer's chest in the way he had when he was putting other people down as being peasants.

Spencer strips down to his underpants and T-shirt. He is surprised at how modest he is in the company of his father, but then this is one of the few equalities between them: the physical proximity of each makes the other equally uncomfortable.

His father winces and shifts and extricates from beneath himself the room key that Spencer had dropped on to the seat of the armchair. Deftly he tosses it on to the table where they play backgammon and settles, as comfortably as his back and neck and digestion will allow, to watch the television. Spencer hurries to retrieve the key. He had been conditioned by his mother never to place a key on a table. Defiant boy Spencer would walk under ladders, refuse to throw salt over his left shoulder after he had spilled it, open umbrellas willy-nilly and carefree indoors. But despite his (father-learned) contempt for superstitions, he has never been able to accept a key on a table.

He washes his face and hands and rubs some water against his teeth and gums.

'We're going to need some things,' he calls out to his father. 'Toothpaste and so forth.'

His father does not reply. He has found some boxing on the TV. He sits in the armchair as he is accustomed to do at home, watching the screen with a look that is almost flirtatious, his chin sunk to his chest so he has to lift his eyes as high as they will go, demure and vulnerable.

'I guess hygiene can wait till the morning. Which bed do you want?' Spencer asks.

His father doesn't seem to hear. He sits, mouth open, as if frozen, while two middleweights in a Las Vegas arena foxily circle each other, shadow-image brothers, one white, the other black, each with a left glove raised to protect his chin, the right held loose and low, ready for an opening.

Spencer gets into the bed that is further from the television. The commentary is horribly loud. He closes his eyes and pulls the covers over his head and, muffled, he continues to be attacked by names and numbers (*Billy Boy Gardel, fourteen and three . . . Juan Riviera, second-round KO four times . . .*), and the trained modulations of a commentator who is trying to arouse his listeners into appreciation of the suspense of the spectacle.

'Would you mind turning down the volume a little?'

Spencer's father does nothing and for one awful moment in which horror and fright mingle with a kind of dazed, fatalistic relief, Spencer is convinced that his father is dead.

He gets up again, and half totters, half runs to the armchair. His father's eyes are open, unblinking. His arms and hands, which had always represented power and unassailable authority to Spencer, have no tone and hardly any substance.

'Dad?'

Nothing. No response. Spencer reaches for the remote control, which is on the right arm of his father's chair, and his father, jealously, sharply, pulls it tight to his own body.

'The volume. Could you turn the volume down a little?'

His father slowly closes his mouth and opens it again as he continues to stare at the TV. Lightly, almost girlishly, he farts.

Spencer tries sleep again, he is exhausted, he is jet-lagged, he has big days ahead of him, he is in the unaccustomed position of having responsibility for his father, he needs sleep more than anything. He strains for it and then tries to relax into it. He holds the spare pillow over his ears against the boxing commentary and tries to bore himself into sleep.

He struggles to recollect the names of every child in his first class of secondary school. But in the hypnagogic zone between wakefulness and slumber, red mocking images of the day—his stepmother, Officer Porrelli, the Cheesequake rest stop—jeer into his closed-eyed vision like a gang of thugs invading a yoga retreat. On his second turn around the classroom, worrying if it was really Nathan Hunt who sat next to Alfred Jesudasen, he succeeds in surrendering to sleep. He dreams about the death and funeral of Muhammad Ali. And his consciousness is again penetrated by the noise of the TV. His eyes open again. His father sits as before, shielded by the dark, staring at the screen, while two semi-naked men try to destroy each other. Spencer gets out of bed. He puts on his jeans and T-shirt and sneakers.

'I'm going downstairs, I think there's a shop downstairs,' he tells his father. 'Get some toothpaste and so forth.'

'Dentures. Denture soap,' his father says.

'Toothpaste for your dentures? Sure. I'll pick some up.'

The hotel is preferable at night. It is less lurid. The brown corridor down to the elevator bank is sort of peaceful. The rattle of the ice-maker makes a pleasant percussion. Spencer rides the elevator to the first floor in the company of two large young men with their petite hairsprayed girlfriends. They are all drunk and have either just had sex or are just about to. Spencer again feels the absence of his camera.

'Have a good night,' he says to them when the elevator doors open.

The girls giggle. The louder of the men says,

'You too, sir.'

'Thank you,' Spencer says and is childishly gratified by this unexpected courtesy.

In the casino shop he buys a large bottle of water, three pairs of underpants, two toothbrushes and two toothpastes, Colgate and Dent-kind, from the small oriental woman who can barely reach over the counter to serve him. And now, he can't resist it, he wanders along the casino floor. He wishes he had his noise-reducing headphones with him, to protect his ears and sensibilities against the clangour and ching of the slot machines. Instead he has his father's watch. If he were in the street, he would be feeling exposed and vulnerable, hiding his wrist against the avarice and bad intentions of strangers. But one of the tricks to get through life is to present the opposite of whatever you are feeling.

He has nearly a hundred dollars in a back pocket of his jeans, two toothbrushes peeping rakishly out of his souvenir store shopping bag, a gold eighteen-carat watch squeezed on to his left wrist. His senses are both dulled and alert, which maybe accounts for him falling for the tricks of casino designers and taking the wrong route towards the elevator bank and finding himself instead at the threshold of the card room.

The key to winning at poker, both online and off—and how Spencer mourns the absence of his laptop, which he hopes is in the trunk of the car and not left behind to the malice of his stepmother at his father's apartment—is game selection. You do not join a game where the players engage in barely secret complicities and collusions. You do not take on strong opposition when you're tired. You do not play with money you cannot afford to lose.

Spencer breaks all these rules, and more. He could just about afford the one dollar-two dollar no-limit hold'em game, but pride or, more likely, vanity pushes him to sit short-stacked at two-five. These are regulars he is up against, the graveyard shift, soft-playing each other, taking it in turns to fleece the tourists, of whom Spencer finds himself the sole representative. He plays up to the role, fumbling with his chips, asking the dealer to clarify the action, sitting looking nervous and concerned, which is almost not an act.

'I'll see you,' he chooses to say when the correct term is 'call'—and he enjoys the pitiless looks that pass between the regulars.

He is given credit for betting his hands, so, squinting at the board, rechecking his cards when the third club arrives on the turn, he makes a trembling raise of the original bet, which had come from the stern little Latino wearing a red-and-white car repairs cap. The Latino nods, flicks his cards away to the dealer, and Spencer gathers the chips and fumblingly arranges them in faltering little towers.

'Where you from, buddy?' says the player to his left, who acts the part of an expansive fellow—it just so happens he was born with the shrewd eyes of the operator who can assess the odds and costs of any situation.

'Uh, London,' Spencer says.

'Nice,' the expansive fellow says.

Spencer endures a conversation about weather, the royal family and exchange rates. He wants to sit quietly, but already the poker magic is doing its work. The world is shrinking to almost the dimensions of the table. These could be the only people in the world, the lady dealer with her apple-pie manner, expansive fellow and stern Latino and the other local grinders, who sit patiently as if they are just passing the time of day, as if they were not a breed of predator waiting for openings, the sniff of blood, the smell of weakness, sharks idly cruising, barely opening their mouths for the fish to come swimming in.

One of the local grinders, a man who displays a small excess of every physical detail, the thickness of his glasses, the straggliness of his beard, the double sniff he gives at the ends of his sentences, asks the expansive fellow about his recent trip to Vegas.

'What about Candace? She give you any trouble?'

'She wanted to go shopping and she wanted to go to shows.'

'So?'

'I did not want to do these things. And how was I going to earn the money to pay for our vacation?'

'Yeah. That's right.'

'Valium's the answer, I recommend it. I'd just put these three Valium in her breakfast orange juice and go downstairs and play cards. She'd wake up in time for me to take her to dinner and a show. She must have slept thirty hours out of forty-two. Said it was the most relaxing time. I'll raise.'

Spencer had stayed out of expansive fellow's way so far. But he decides it is time to get involved.

'How much is it?'

'To you, my friend, fifteen dollars, no discount.'

'OK. I'll see you.'

Spencer wonders whether he is laying it on a bit thick, this performance of nervously ignorant incapacity, his poker solecisms, but it had always been a failing with him to act out of aversion to the obvious. Oftentimes the obvious choice is the right one.

And he wonders whether he is sitting in on his own future. He could become one of these old sharks, in a card room anywhere in the world, taking advantage of the tourists and the young, grinding out a kind of living, getting fatter and iller and airless. He has never been a nature boy. Apart from an affinity to donkeys and tortoises, the organic world makes him uncomfortable.

As if the result of the hand is foreordained, the locals chat away during it. Straggly fellow asks expansive fellow if he is going to be playing the big tournament. It becomes clear that the only reason he asked the question is so he can announce that he won a satellite entry to it.

Spencer bumbles his way to the end of the hand, without ever consulting his hole cards. He checks when the expansive fellow checks, calls when he bets. At the river, his opponent smilingly puts in a larger bet that Spencer reads as a bluff.

'Can I raise?' he asks the dealer.

'You can do what you like, darling, so long as it's legal.'

'He can do a lot more than that, I heard, Rose-Mary.'

'You hush your mouth Lloyd.'

'I'll raise,' Spencer says.

'How much, darling? You have to make it an amount.'

'Oh. All of it. I'll go all-in.'

'I call,' Lloyd says.

The board shows ace of hearts, three of clubs, king of diamonds, four of spades, three of hearts.

Lloyd tables his cards, ace-king, giving him top two pair.

Spencer turns over his own two cards, expecting nothing beyond the reproach for trying to be fancy when he is preoccupied and sleepless and poor. He has the six and three of spades, making an unlikely three of a kind.

'I got a bit lucky there,' Spencer says.

Sleep is always more available following a victory than a defeat. Spencer, unable not to follow certain rules of etiquette, particularly if they are related to poker, stays at the table for a polite twenty minutes before returning to his room.

His sleeping father is puffing out his cheeks and blowing, as he used to do in moments of impatience or stress. Spencer fans out his winnings on the bedside table, and lies in his bed, falls asleep to the lullaby of the thuds of music from the room next door and the sounds his father makes at night, the rumbles and snores and sharp catches for air, and the muttering that has no clear cause or resolution.

In the morning, Dwight has a surprise for them.

'Gentlemen! A superior mode of perambulation!'

Interrupting their arduous journey back from the All-You-Can-Eat! breakfast death-buffet, Spencer and his father make their way to the front desk. Dwight places a finger against his lips like a parent at Christmas trying to still the anticipation of a child.

'Shut your eyes please, no peeking.'

Spencer's father dutifully closes his eyes. Spencer keeps his eyes open, with arms ready to catch his father if he should fall.

'De-*da*!'

And in front of them is a motorised wheelchair, gleaming silver and black, its engine gently purring.

'Allow me to regale you with some its specifications. Puncture-proof tyres, easily foldable for transport and storage, manual freewheel function, battery range twenty-two miles, cushioned upholstery for extra comfort, powerful rear drive delivers excellent power and acceleration, swivel seat with reclining device and safety belt, off-board charger, maximum speed fourteen miles per hour. What do you think of this baby?'

Spencer's father still has his eyes tightly, patiently, closed.

'Uh, sir? You can look now.'

Spencer's father opens his eyes and squints and focuses. Spencer expects a graceless response and is not disappointed.

'How much you burning me for?'

Dwight has the grace not to be offended.

'*Gratis*, Mister L, all part of the hospitality. Pro bono. Please.

Asseyez-vous. Investigate the potential and capacity of the power-chaise.'

Spencer's father deigns to lower himself into the chair. Gingerly, he taps a button on the control pad and the chair whizzes into the front desk, inscribing two neat dents with its aluminium footrests. He taps the opposing button and whizzes backwards, scattering an early morning cleaner, who performs an impressive leap of escape, using his floor mop as a pole to vault with.

'There may be a requisite orientation period,' Dwight allows.

Spencer's father executes a sharp turn, a burst of speed towards the glass doors that lead on to the Boardwalk, another turn, a barely controlled figure-of-eight that leaves him breathless through his oxygen tube, and he is back at the front desk, his silver hair flapping wild.

'Beautiful. I thank you. You're a good man,' he says.

The oxygen cylinder travels in the front basket. Spencer's father zooms away again, heading towards the outside world, the ocean. Spencer jogs behind, the latest message from Michelle in his hand, struggling to keep up. His father makes no allowances for anyone of a slower pace, or even for physical obstacles. If it were not for a stranger's hand, opening the plate-glass door to the Boardwalk, allowing his father to leave the building unimpeded, Spencer would have had to spend the rest of the morning picking glass out of his father's wounds.

The day is lovely, spring sunshine, soft breeze, boating weather. Spencer had been about to ask his father whether he misses his boating days, but he is still chugging behind and his words would be lost between them, and anyway he is becoming mistrustful of these conversations that begin with *Do you miss . . . ?* and *Do you remember . . . ?* and *What was the name of . . . ?* What is transacted between them should be about here, now, this day, us. Spencer despises flashback.

When his father consents finally to pause, stopping at the wooden ramp that crosses the beach to the ocean, he wipes his brow with his handkerchief and grins at Spencer.

'You want to go down to the sea?' Spencer asks.

Carefully, the wheels of his father's chair churning up sparkles of sand, they make their way to the water's edge. His father removes his surgical collar and, before Spencer can protest or intervene, the oxygen nozzles from his nose. He breathes in deep, he shuts his eyes, he opens them wide, a kind of ecstasy.

Spencer tries to reach the same feeling or at least make an approach to it. He breathes in and out, letting things drop away. He aims for utter thoughtlessness; his father is teaching him something here, the value of the moment, the air and sunshine on his skin, just to be. But Jimmy Ludwig operates on a schedule that allows no time for Spencer's nirvana.

'Come on. Turn me around.'

They make the climb back up to the Boardwalk.

'Don't fuss,' his father says as Spencer hops behind him to pull away a plastic bag that has become wrapped around a wheel of his chair.

They promenade along the Boardwalk, the casinos on their right, the ocean on their left. They pass other, dissimilar couples, middle-aged husbands and wives, rickshaw riders killing time visiting each other in their cabs, drunks and junkies sharing cigarettes. Spencer suggests that they try a game of crazy golf, but the shape of the course would be difficult for a wheelchair to traverse and anyway Jimmy Ludwig has his eye on a more glamorous sport.

'You got the balls?' he says.

Spencer's father pulls up at the ticket office of an outdoor go-kart arena.

'Sure,' Spencer doubtfully says. 'But are you going to be able to manage a go-kart?'

'Who needs a go-kart?' Jimmy says.

And it is true. Some of the other customers complain, but a twenty-dollar bill slipped to the custodian works wonders. The rest of the track is cleared, leaving the course clear for Spencer and Jimmy. Spencer has some initial difficulties with his kart, it stutters beneath him, but inspired by the sight of his father in his wheelchair zipping around the course, racing through the hairpin bend, the caroms and skids, he plucks up the courage to push his kart into top gear and catch up.

He tries to pass his father going into the widest bend, past where the custodian stands, but his father swings from side to side, blocking Spencer each time. One moment Spencer thinks he has him, he draws almost level, Jimmy Ludwig leaning over his handlebars, his face utterly cold and fierce, until he wrenches his wheelchair to the side to sideswipe his son. Spencer pulls out of the collision at the last moment, kicks down at the brake, sending himself into a spin that he manages to come out of with only one bounce into the safety wall of stacked tyres.

His father is nearly half a lap ahead. Spencer, renewed, speeds back on to the circuit, never touching the brake. Jimmy Ludwig is growing complacent up ahead, relaxing his vigilance, looking from side to side, the line of disgruntled children waiting for their turn, seagulls swooping over the pier, the dull daylight anti-glitter of casinos.

Spencer has his chance on the final lap, entering the stretch of straight track going towards the finishing line. He leans over his wheel, coaxing every possibility of speed out of his machine. His father is slowing down, one hand on the handlebar, the other casually resting in his lap.

'Coming to get you!'

Spencer's shout alarms his father, whose smile of pleasure is replaced by confusion, he pulls the wheelchair in one direction, then the other, it topples slowly towards its side, rolling only on its left wheels, Spencer is level with his father now, he could go past him if he chose, he wants the taste of this fine victory, the finishing line is ahead, the custodian waves a tired chequered flag. Spencer's father bumps back on to all four wheels again, is jolted against the handlebars, bounces once. He shakes his head, winces at the pain this causes in his back and neck. Spencer slows his go-kart and stops beside his father.

'Are you OK?' he asks.

Jimmy ruefully rubs his neck.

'I'll be all right,' he says.

'Are you sure?'

'Absolutely.'

He is not entirely all right: something is affecting him. He rubs his neck, he puts his hands back on the handlebars. He looks at the sky and Spencer looks up with him.

'But—'

But Spencer's words are interrupted by the sound of the wheelchair whirring into action again, and his father looks back at him with sneaky sly triumph as he races to the finishing line to take the chequered flag. The watching children cheer and clap, not entirely ironically, which Jimmy Ludwig acknowledges with a crisp military salute.

Spencer putters after him. He can hardly begrudge his father this victory, even if it was won by using Spencer's good nature against him.

Their Atlantic City idyll continues. They buy milk shakes at an ice-cream parlour that is decorated with images from the Monopoly board. They eat pizza on a Boardwalk bench. They drink margaritas and play low-stakes blackjack at a casino decorated like a Wild West saloon. They both win, twenty dollars to Spencer, thirty dollars to his father. A fat man runs across the casino floor and Spencer and his father watch his bulky elegant process and they both make the same shape with their mouths. Jimmy Ludwig rests a fatherly hand on his son's shoulder and Spencer feels about ten years old. Or seventeen, or three, or forty-two.

'I've just had a revelation,' Spencer says.

'A what?'

'Revelation. An epiphany.'

His father's hand drops away. He shakes his head in incomprehension.

Their dealer falters as he delivers a second five to Spencer's hand. His eyes meet Spencer's. Dealing cards on behalf of the casino, delivering up his humanity for wages to become part of the machinery that so efficiently separates poor people from their money—who will meanwhile tip the instrument of their own destruction—might lead someone of a vaguely spiritual bent to develop a hunger for epiphany and revelation.

'I'll hit,' Spencer says.

The dealer nods, flicks an ace to Spencer.

'Soft twenty-one,' he says.

'I'll stand.'

The dealer has a four. Spencer's father makes the correct decision to stand on thirteen. The dealer deals himself a king and then a seven. Twenty-one.

'Disgusting,' Spencer's father says.

'Sir?' the dealer says.

'I think we'll sit out the next hand. Thank you.'

Spencer tosses a red five-dollar chip to the dealer, who catches it expertly, raps it against the table and drops it into his gratuities tin.

'Thank you sir,' he says, fixing upon Spencer a look of utter hate that might be the product of a sense of self that requires larger tips than five dollars, or the deprivation felt by the spiritual seeker who has been thwarted on the road to his enlightenment.

Spencer and his father gather up their chips and leave the blackjack table.

'Let's sit here a while,' Spencer says.

It's the Sports Book. Banks of television monitors show

baseball games, basketball, horse racing, ice hockey. A large screen displays lists of names and numbers that are indecipherable to Spencer beyond a recognition that they have something to do with competition and odds. He always finds the Sports Book the most tranquil place in a casino. In Las Vegas, he would sometimes sit for hours in the Sports Book to read and write. *The Captain's Grief* was written in the Sports Book of the Mirage. When Spencer had his greatest poker triumph, going deep and cashing in the Main Event of the World Series of Poker, the Sports Book of the Rio was his resting zone.

'What were you saying?' Spencer's father asks. He rubs his eyes. He yawns. He takes off his surgical collar, placing it in the wire basket at the front of his wheelchair, and his head sinks down further.

'You should have a rest. We should go back to our room and you should have a rest.'

'I'm not hungry,' Spencer's father says.

'No. I know. But we've done a lot already and you haven't taken your medications.'

'Bullshit,' Spencer's father says.

'I'm inclined to agree with you. But anyway, I've got an interview to do this afternoon. Magazine interview. I should get back to the hotel.'

Spencer's father doesn't quite grasp the substance of what Spencer is saying but he takes from it the meaning that Spencer is using his frailties as an excuse for something that he wants to do that excludes him.

'Bullshit,' he says again.

And Spencer is returned again to the child whose throat would raw at the intimation of a severe word from his father, whose eyes would well with tears at the slightest harshness from his father. In summer, Mary always sneezes when she walks into the sunlight. It means nothing, just a reflex. Spencer used to try telling himself that his fragile response to his father's words was just a reflex too, but he could never believe that to be true.

'When I'm with you,' he says, 'sometimes I feel very grown up and sometimes I feel like the most dependent child.'

'You want some money?' his father says.

'No. I don't.'

'Well you should!'

Jimmy Ludwig crumbles, his faith in money sustains. And this is at the crux of Spencer's revelation. We are a jumble of competing, accidental selves, and our sense of continuity is in the constancy of our feelings. When Spencer fell out of love with Mary's mother, he became a different person. When his father dies, Spencer will grieve for a man he used to be.

Jimmy Ludwig has an enviable constancy. He has always believed in himself and, ever since the War at least, he has always believed in money.

And what does Spencer have, beyond the influences he was born to? The films he's made, the films he is going to make, his daughter, and maybe more important than anything, movie moments made by others, the particular images that have occupied and shaped his internal landscape.

'What happened to your friend? How's she doing?'

'Which friend?'

Spencer knows perfectly well who his father is asking about. Few aspects of his life registered with his father, even before he suffered his stroke. And his father likes very few people. His attitude to other people is predicated on the disappointment he expects to receive from them. But he liked Rick Violet. He had pronounced him charming.

'Your friend. She able to get you any work?'

'She probably could. If I asked.'

'Then you should ask.'

His father's logic is inevitably faultless. It just does not allow for emotion.

'I need to go my own way,' Spencer says.

'Bullshit,' his father says. 'The poor despise the rich.'

'Really? Is that the way it is?'

'That's the way it is.'

'Maybe I just reject all that. Maybe I reject money!'

A few faces glance dully at them in the Sports Book, but emotion can hardly compete with sports betting and they look back to the big screens again.

Spencer's father shakes his head even though it costs him pain to do so.

After they had made their third film together, Spencer was the coming man. He had displayed his gifts, unshowily, in the service of art. He could write, edit, direct, produce. Rick had been the nominal director, but everyone knew that Spencer's was the talent that lay behind it all. That summer after film school, warmed in the glory of his achievement, the aura of his future that was already being written, lazily half listening to offers of work while he waited for *it*, the real job, his great expectation, which arrived, as he knew it would, it was all understood—the world was a place of straight lines, unbroken promises and clear directions—a feature-film adaptation of a story he loved, Julio Cortázar's *House Taken Over*, to be made with American money but no interference.

The producer—a rakish young Londoner who worked in LA, and had already become his friend, they understood each other so well—invited Spencer to take part in a cricket match. The night before the game, Spencer was called by the producer. The team was a man short, could Spencer suggest anyone? Generously, already feeling sentimental about his former colleague whom he was leaving behind, Spencer brought Rick Violet to the game.

Spencer had been a good cricketer, a pugnacious middle-order batsman, a crafty spin bowler, a decent fielder. He knew how to play cricket. Rick, though, was something special. He played with elegance and ease, a public-school grace. After the game, the team's captain, Spencer's new patron and producer, asked for Rick's number.

'It's the Hollywood Exiles, they always beat us. With your mate in the team we'll take them this year. Cheers, Spence. We'll be talking soon.'

Spencer, in his supposedly charmed naivety, had passed on the number, glad to be helping out. And he never heard from his new employer and friend again. Spencer was not given the job; Rick was. So a team of actor dilettantes could be beaten in a game of cricket, Rick Violet was put on the path that had been meant for Spencer. As they say in the poker world, it is better to be lucky than good.

'You tired?' Spencer asks. 'Maybe we should go back.'

His father ignores him. He stops a passing waitress and asks her for a bowl of cereal. He might not want a bowl of cereal but that is what he is going to get.

While Spencer was still at film school, he worked with a Marxist collective, Cinema Praxis. The group was a funded (BFI, Channel 4, trade unions) leftover from a previous age. It believed in revolution, the eventual withering-away of the state, an advance guard of intellectuals exposing the contradictions of capitalism, raising the consciousness of the oppressed working class. Spencer carried a boom microphone while the leader of the group, a grey-bearded Alsatian who had done something glamorous and dangerous in the 1968 Paris riots, barked questions in parlour rooms in Keighley and Nottingham at miners who had lost their jobs.

'If you're not a communist when you're a teenager then there's something wrong with you,' his father had said.

When Spencer's father was seventeen he was a boy communist, a disaffected, malcontentish type of youth. He and his friend Benny sneaked across the border, leaving behind German-occupied Poland for a dreamed-of utopia. Life was here, and yet it was elsewhere. If they made it to Moscow for the May Day celebrations of 1940, then they would find the promised land.

Four months later, he was on a train heading for Siberia. A foreign parasite, he was sentenced to eight years' hard labour in a prison camp. His job in the workers' paradise was to build railway tracks.

The women in the camp over the fence tried to entice the men across. They offered them inducements for sex. They stood at their glassless windows, lifted their smocks and exposed their breasts.

'They promised us food,' Spencer's father says. 'They stood at the windows with their smocks lifted up. They masturbated with salt stuffed into a sock.'

The shocking thing to Spencer is not the image of lascivious women standing at windows with their smocks lifted above their breasts, the Siberian cold howling at them as they masturbated with socks filled with salt, or that Spencer's father could recollect the moment, and the image, and the emotion, and the language to describe it, but that he was even talking about the subject. Both of Spencer's parents were, in their different ways, prudes. They did not generally speak about any subject that was unseemly.

Sitting in the Sports Book talking about sex and Siberia, watching a bowl of cereal being delivered by a waitress of Spencer's age dressed as a Roman slave girl, Spencer realises that he is scratching the skin of his ankle beneath his sock and abruptly stops doing so. Even if the casino allowed filming to take place, which he doubts—casinos are as notoriously coy as latrophobes about showing their insides—Spencer would not want anything he made to look as uninspired and cold as a Cinema Praxis documentary.

'A cinema audience,' Spencer says, 'wants, in fact it *deserves*, some spectacle. It's a perversity not to give it.'

'Sure,' his father says.

'The *now*, that's something films can do. Make something happen in the now. And if we're honest with ourselves, most of our favourite films have someone we fancy in them, erotic pull, that's what movies are good for. The audience knows what rooms look like, they spend most of their time in them. Life's got enough boredom in it without film-makers inflicting more.'

'Absolutely.'

'So it's lack of imagination and generosity masquerading as some bogus kind of authenticity to inflict so-called naturalism on them. But at the same time we can't have an enactment. That would be the worst kind of schlock, sepia-stained footage of over-enthusiastic actresses doing grimy stuff with socks. That's how you become Ken Russell or Lina Wertmuller.'

His father has eaten as much of his cereal as he is able. He pushes the bowl away, watches with little interest the swirl of milk lapping up against the sides.

'You know what I mean? Real guignol stuff. Orgasmic expressions, shots of thighs beaded with sweat, vulvas through the bars, pan around to the solitary prisoner standing in the snow, empty food bowl forgotten in his hand, gazing upon the spectacle not even with longing, just looking into something that he has lost, something that used to make him a man.'

'I mean, it's impossible isn't it? A film can't do that, it doesn't know how to show pain, it just becomes picturesque. What we want is the audience to feel what you felt—at least with you talking, here, now, we get some sense of who you are even if we'll never get hold of the person you used to be.'

'Sorry about that,' his father says quite cheerily.

'It's OK. It's not your fault,' Spencer says.

Briefly he wonders what his father might be apologising for and why he is so reflexively quick to forgive. He wonders too why he is so ready to cover up with noise moments when things might be revealed.

'I'm a victim of my times,' he tells his father. 'Nothing as dramatic as what happened to you. But just the same a *zeitgeist* blew through us both. You had a brutal scarred Europe, fascism, dictators, death camps, and I had . . . You know, you'll find this funny. I not only used to think that cinema can change lives, I also thought that it could tell the truth. Or at least reveal it. Do you remember . . .?'

'Remember what?' his father says.

It could be Warsaw or Siberia or Monte Cassino, or what it was like to be suddenly demobbed in Cardiff in 1946, or looking for your family in Italian Displaced Persons Camps in 1945, only to find that all of them were dead, or why you were such a bad husband to my mother and a bad father to me. And do you remember telling me once that you would have met my mother anyway, without war or the intercession of history? That it was meant to be, two Polish-Jewish families, a rebellious son, a wistful daughter, they would have found each other . . . And do you remember why you said this? Was it an expression of romance or just trying to make Spencer feel good about something, maybe even himself; was it just like the time you pretended to believe in God for the benefit of your son, believing that a father's influence should be allowed to go just so far and that there were some things a man must decide for himself? And do you remember the person you used to be?

And do you remember what it was like when you won your first case?—there's a photo of you, presumably taken by Spencer's mother, outside the courthouse, and there's no triumph in your face, just impatience, either for the next, bigger case to begin, or for the rendezvous with the cute stenographer in the bar around the corner, or for the photograph-taking to be over.

It is the worst kind of weakness. Sit with an old person, smooth the blanket across their knees and ask them to remember. Of course they remember. Just as it is safe to ask anyone upper-class about their family and sit back and let the anecdotes come, you can ask an old person to dribble out some memory. And they will tell you a story from the War or the factory or about someone they used to know, who might be, as far as the listener can tell, an old friend or a politician or television star or someone glimpsed one day through a train carriage window.

The old are becakked with memory, they spill out the stuff incontinently, which is maybe why Spencer despises flashback. *That* is not what is important, *this* is what is important. This thing we are making together, the squeezing together of the old gentleman's hands, the look on the girl's face, the shape of her neck, the sun's reflection on the windows of a black glass building, that movement you make towards me, these are the beautiful things. They are more or less worthless if you can only understand them with backstory.

There are things that Spencer would like to know. Some of them might even be meaningful. And Spencer believes that there are stories that should not die, that should pass down the generations with a greater intrinsic value than money. But Spencer and his father exist in the now. If his father is to persist in time, if the two of them are going to perform anything valuable together, then it is the *now* they are pursuing, not some finished *then*.

It is go-kart racing, blackjack in the Wild West, not memories of Siberia.

Death by food in the buffet. Taking the all-you-can-eat dare.

His father looks at the empty place on his wrist where his watch used to be.

'Well, it's been nice,' he says, pushing at the table to get his unsteady body to rise.

Chapter Six

Spencer's interview is imminent. The journalist, who has a sweet fresh voice that makes Spencer think of drum majorettes, Tuesday Weld, of girls in 1960s movies who wear white patent-leather boots and miniskirts, calls Spencer's room from the lobby.

'The festival has a room for interviews, but I can come up,' she says. 'Whichever is best for you.'

Spencer takes a quick look around the room, its disshev-elled state, which mirrors his own, the plastic bags from the casino shop, the rumble and hiss of his father's oxygen machine, boxing on the TV, tissues on the floor, and his father, who sits on the edge of his unmade bed in baggy white briefs and high black socks, his stomach pulling out and in with each laboured breath.

'I'll come down. It's probably easier,' Spencer says.

His father ignores him, which he usually does when there is boxing to watch. Spencer stands for a moment in front of the bathroom mirror, pats down his hair, smooths down his T-shirt, puts on his jacket, double-checks he has the room key. He feels light and nervous, as if for a date.

But when Spencer leaves the room, his father tags along too, wearing just his underpants and socks.

'Where are we going?' he asks.

'I've got an interview. And you're going nowhere looking like that.'

He dresses his father, feels an unrequired lurch of sympathy for his stepmother while doing so. And together they make their way down to the elevator and the lobby.

Tuesday Weld is not waiting for him. The woman who approaches them is inside a shapeless black T-shirt and baggy black jeans that Spencer tries not to recognise as a variant of his own dress code. She wears large glasses and carries two handfuls of plastic bags—the Bongo African Grocery, Boom Supermarket, the United Adult Book Store.

She tries to offer him a hand to shake through the jumble of her bags.

'I'm Jenny De Soto. From *Film Culture*.'

'Spencer Ludwig. From London.'

'And is *this* . . .?'

'No,' Spencer wearily says. 'It's not a leading Albanian film-maker. It's—'

'I wouldn't have thought so. I was going to say, is this your father?'

'It is actually. Jenny De Soto, Jimmy Ludwig. Dad, this lady is from a magazine.'

Nervously, Spencer awaits the expression of disdain that his father inevitably displays when meeting an unkempt female. For poor people, Spencer's father has a little sympathy, because he was once poor himself. Women who eschew any attempt at glamour he finds distasteful, as if they have chosen to wear their lack of moral value on their bodies. In this case, though, perhaps out of loyalty to the situation, however he understands it, and to Spencer, he puts on his old-world charm, which most women, even intelligent ones, find peculiarly affecting.

'It's delightful to meet you,' he says.

'And you, sir. There's something so much alike about the two of you. It's a pleasure to meet you both. Shall we set up? There's a room set aside.'

'Let me just dispose of my father. So to speak.'

Spencer gives his father $110 from his poker winnings and steers him past the slot machines to the $5 minimum black-jack table. His father docilely sits down, exchanges the money, and before Spencer can witness what happens to the entire stack of chips that his father confidently slides on to his betting box, he demands from him the promise that he won't move from this area, and returns to the lobby to follow Jenny De Soto to the film festival interview room.

'Your father's delightful,' she says as she extricates cassette recorder and notebook and two pens (biros, one black, one blue) from three different bags.

'Is he? Thank you. I haven't seen one of those for a while.'

'The tape machine? It works.'

'I'm sure it does. I'm sorry, I hadn't meant to . . .'

He is taking the wrong tone. If he were Rick Violet, or even his father, he would be charming his interviewer, making her feel as if she were the only woman in his world.

She picks up her pens with the delicacy that some over-weight people possess and holds them out for him to see.

'You remember . . .?' she says.

His mind is blank. She is referring to something specific here, something she wants to be shared.

'*Gold Treatment*,' she says to prompt him.

'Oh. Yes. Sorry. Very good.'

In that film, an early short, the main character, an architect who refuses to make the compromise of constructing a building, has a fetish for Bic biros.

'It's probably that I'm not used to being interviewed by someone who is actually familiar with my work,' he says.

'Oh I can't believe that!'

She admires his films, she knows them very well, and as the conversation goes on, the claims she makes for his work are just what he would hope for an ideal audience to apprehend. He should not judge her; he is no oil painting himself, so why shouldn't a bulky woman with supermarket bags be his audience angel?

'Your films are numinous.'

'Luminous?'

'Numinous.'

'Numerous?'

'Numinous.'

'Oh.'

It is one of those words that he has learned and then forgotten again; he vaguely supposes it to refer to something religious but he isn't sure what.

'Uh. Thank you,' he says.

'What are your plans?'

'To make some money.'

He has disappointed her.

'But . . .?! If you wanted to make money, if you wanted to sell out, then you could have done that years ago.'

'I could?'

'With your gifts you could have turned your hand to anything. It's obvious. Look. For example, you say here . . .' She rummages in her bags, pulls out snatches of paper, which she glances over, stuffs back in again. '. . . well somewhere, I read an interview where you said you would never make a commercial. We think that's wonderful.'

'We?'

'Your fans.'

He does not think of himself as having fans. His world

doesn't allow for the notion of consequence. Each time he embarks on a film, he is making a film for the very first time to an entirely new audience.

'But,' she says, and she rubs her face quite hard as if she has to punish herself for her temerity in beginning a question with a possible objection. 'But.'

'But what?' he asks, feeling playful.

'But. About the, you know, well, *it*. I was surprised. Of course, there's nothing wrong with it, per se, but given what you'd said and so forth and therefore, and . . .'

'I'm sorry. I don't understand what you're asking.'

'OK. OK. That's OK. Let's move on. Who do you make your films for?'

'Me, I suppose.'

'Isn't that kind of selfish?'

'I don't mean it quite like that. In a way, the films I make are the films I would like to see. So it's not like I have some ideal audience in mind, the little lady in Ongar or anything like that. They have to stand for something, they have to be new, they have to be the sort of thing that I would want to see, that I've *never* seen.'

'That's wonderful.'

'Is it?'

'It's *exactly* what I would have hoped you'd say. Well not *exactly*, because I wouldn't have found the right language for the idea if you know what I mean.'

Does what he is saying actually accord to the truth or just to the overgenerous conceptions she has of him?—or could he just tell her anything and she would incorporate it into the dreams she has for him and his work and therefore, presumably, herself?

'And who do you admire?'

'You mean directors? The usual suspects, Dreyer, Nick Ray, Fassbinder and Bresson of course, John Ford. Bertolucci before he stopped being a Marxist. Buñuel, except I've always thought there was something fishy about him. But I think what we need to realise is that it's the work that's important, not who made it. Trust the song, not the singer, you know what I mean? So we can love *Simon of the Desert* or *The Conformist* or *In a Lonely Place* without having to bother about what Buñuel's relationship to religion was or Bertolucci's aestheticisation of revolution or how cruel and fucked-up a man Nicholas Ray was.'

Give Spencer Ludwig a rapt appreciative audience and he becomes loquacious. His thought processes achieve a suppleness and fluidity. His sentences become prose. For a moment, in her appreciation of him, in what it enables him to be, she becomes beautiful.

'Well yes. Uh huh. OK. I get it. But I was really thinking more of people working in the present day. Almodóvar, for example. Dee Selby. And Rick Violet, of course.'

And how his spirits sink.

'Why of course?'

'Well. Just. I don't know, you know. Rick Violet.'

All roads lead to Rick Violet. It would not surprise him to walk out of this room and see a hundred-foot poster advertising Rick Violet, to step outside into the Boardwalk chill and find it has been renamed Violet Way.

'To be honest—and this goes against what I've just been saying—but I went off him a bit after his conviction.'

'*Conviction?*'

'I'm sorry. I shouldn't have mentioned that. Let's get back to your question.'

'Conviction? Are you talking about a criminal conviction?'

'No no, let's forget about it. He's hushed it up very successfully and I shouldn't have mentioned it, it's bad of me.'

Worse than she can possibly know, this casual action of petty vindictive malice.

'I'm very surprised. I mean, we've heard rumours, but . . .'

'No. I'm sorry. It's awful of me to mention it. Let's talk about contemporary film directors. Remind me again what you wanted to know. Dee Selby, yes, is very good. I'm a big fan of her work.'

She is flustered again, as she had been at the beginning, before he had put her at her ease, or, more accurately, before they had found an accord in each other's company.

In his left jacket pocket are the messages from Michelle that Dwight has given him. Each is more beseeching than the last, and each would deliver a promise should he have chosen to receive it. He has glanced at numbers with zeros, multiple exclamation marks, and the words *Please* and *SPENCER!* and *You can* and *They will* before crumpling them up and adding them to his pocket, which now bulges with the irregular paper balls of Michelle's entreaties.

Perhaps this is the time to read them, spread them out on the table, push Jenny De Soto's cassette recorder to one side, smooth out the pages, the Horseshoe crest of, he cannot think why, a flower and a sword, Dwight's neatly printed writing, *Please call, there is, he has, they want* . . . and he might read them now.

'Would you like me to take you on a tour of the town? You could bring your father.'

For the first time since they embarked upon this trip, he has forgotten about his father. Even playing poker the night before, an occupation that usually obliterates the world, shrinking existence to a narrow arena of felt, the gold watch on his wrist had kept his father close; and during the night his dreams had been full of the image of his father, as they had used to be when he was young and wanted from his night, like every other male adolescent, to dream of adventures and loose women.

'The thing about Atlantic City. It's like Washington, DC. A slum of a town with a bogus city in the middle designed for profiteering and failure.'

'That's very interesting, but I really should check on my father.'

'Oh. Are we done?'

'We're adjourning. I'm just a little concerned. I left him at a blackjack table. He might have lost his money, he might have gone wandering. I don't know.'

'You're very devoted, aren't you?'

'Am I? I don't know about that. We're making a film together.'

Somehow he has acquired her; he waits by the conference-room door for his companion to gather up the tools of her trade.

Michelle's notes plead for him to call her. There are opportunities waiting for him, all he has to do is call her and they are his. In the last one, no doubt desperate, she begins by reminding him of the account outstanding between them. Which is all that Spencer needs to reject her, and perhaps his old world, utterly.

Spencer has been wondering how this might end. If it were a comedy, then it should end with a marriage, he and his father hook up with two hookers, find a wedding chapel, one of these casinos must have one, trying to ape Las Vegas as a destination resort, walk up the aisle, giving each other away, to blushing brides innocent again. If it were a tragedy, then death is the only solution. But this is neither, and both.

It is, he supposes, a road movie. Looking for his father on the casino floor, outside on the Boardwalk, with Jenny De Soto puffing beside him, he fails to find him. This cannot be over yet.

'How,' he asks Jenny De Soto, 'should a road movie end?'

'A road movie?'

'That's right. You understand genre. What are the ways a road movie can end?'

'Uh. I guess there are three different ways.'

'OK. Let's hear them.'

'Or maybe four. Four.'

'OK. And?'

She would have been a smart student, taking notes, understanding the subject with more feel than the professor could ever share, internalising what she thought was required, while the prettier, more popular students chewed gum and went to parties.

'The protagonists learn something from their journey, they achieve what they thought they needed, or they don't, but that doesn't really matter, because along the way they've discovered something more important that they've probably had all along and kind of undervalued, the meaning of friendship, is usually love—it's kind of a Christian form, isn't it? Redemption through picaresque?—and they go back home, and they're wiser, they've learnt something, and now they can accommodate themselves to their previous discontents. *Two for the Road*, you know, the Donen movie?'

'OK. Yeah. Good.'

So Jimmy Ludwig forgives his wife for being the person she is rather than the woman he would want her to be. They can begin to enjoy their twilight of toaster-ovens and day beds together. And Spencer Ludwig returns to London, to what? This road movie can't be nearly over yet, because he has achieved no triumph and neither is he aware of having learned much yet; he just feels tiresomely unaccommodated and peevish.

'Or else the protagonists get married, to each other—*It Happened One Night*.'

'I think we can forget about that one. How about number two?'

'Well number two would be, they discover something at their destination, which they had never thought would be their destination, it's just another place along the way, that's what they'd thought, but something unexpected happens, and this is the place that feels like home. You might have seen? There's a recent Iranian film, called *Nowhere*. It's very beautiful.'

'All right. OK.'

So Spencer and his father will settle here, in Atlantic City. Spencer will take a job with the film festival, or he becomes a poker player, grinding out the hours and the blinds while his father prepares them meals out of eggs. And they live together in a boarding house, or in a casino suite reserved for high-rollers, Dwight tending to every whim, even making sure they cultivate a few more appetites that they have never tasted the consummation of before.

'Number three?'

'That's the usual one, or maybe the second-most usual after number one. You know, they've tasted too much, pushed themselves too far out of reach, and now they can never go home, they've ridden away from any possibility of their former lives, and death is the only available outcome, the road is the pathway to the grave, *Easy Rider*, *Vanishing Point*.'

Spencer, serious now, this has moved beyond the dialectic of the classroom, he sees the last image in a cold way, the father-and-son fireball on the Parkway, or the son washed out to sea, father dying on the casino floor. Or, of course, vice versa.

'Number four?'

'Maybe this is the most usual one. You know, the meaning of the journey is just the taking of it. The trip that can never end? *Five Easy Pieces* and so forth?'

'Yeah. That's right.'

And the movie continues until the camera can no longer keep up with the protagonists, and off they go, Spencer and his father, getting smaller into the distance, disappearing, a speck on the endless road.

'That's very good, Jenny. You know your stuff.'

'Thank you.'

'And why do we like road movies so much?'

His questioning is making her nervous, but it shouldn't do, because she knows. Maybe this is his unlikely culmination, and she has an older sister, or a feisty disabled mother to be suitably companioned to his father, and the four of them will set up house together, in a world of film references and supermarket bags.

'I guess, because they operate in the endless now?'

She is right, and this is the glory and the tedium of the road movie. But how then would he incorporate the significant moments of his father's past? Spencer despises costume drama almost as surely as he despises flashback. The two together would be intolerable, Jimmy Ludwig in pre-War suit—or bring it into the now, make his father's history into a universal one. Jimmy Ludwig in Sarajevo (wearing a not-dissimilar suit), or Kigali (stumbling along a dusty road in bright summer clothes), or Gaza (his vulnerable head wrapped inside a keffiyeh), a Palestinian refugee or a Rwandan, who owns nothing except for a tragedy in his past and an endless hope for his future.

'But tell me, I'm puzzled about something.'

'What's that?'

'Since when did you ever obey the rules of genre?'

It's a good question, and she's probably right, although *Competition*, being a comedy, does end with a wedding. He and Jenny walk, increasingly frantic, in decreasing circles, on Boardwalk casino passageways, back into the Horseshoe, down corridors he's never suspected before.

'Maybe this should be a gambling movie,' he says.

Spencer's father had beaten the odds at three significant moments in his life, so why should a New Jersey coastal resort town be any kind of threat to him? He had been a Jew in German-occupied Warsaw in 1939, a slave labourer in a Siberian prison camp in 1941, a Polish soldier at the battle of Monte Cassino in 1944. Look around you, see the men who will shortly be dead. Your friend Benny, selected by your parents for being a good boy, Benny excelled at school, he had modest, studious ways, and you were such an unreliable boy, you had been through six high schools by the time you were sixteen, you smoked cigarettes, chased after girls, hung water-filled condoms on the blackboard, refused to accept anyone's authority but your own. Your family was a mystery to you. Apart from one cousin, Tosia, with whom on family get-togethers you would steal away and spend an hour or so locked together, mouth to mouth, vigorously kissing until your lips were bruised and sore, you had no understanding of any of them. Not your father, who occupied his own unenviable place with such dull complacency, not your mother, who was hardly saintly in her invalid state, certainly not your brother, who found it so easy to be met with approval. And all those cousins and aunts and uncles, who would shortly be dead.

Now, given the boy you were, so cocky and unsure, so accustomed to disapproval, with your likings for food and girls and your mistrust, your suspicion of anyone's intentions, and your faith that life was elsewhere, that there was a somewhere else, where, if you only could find it, your own life might begin, given all this, it was unlikely that you would take to Benny. Just the fact of him being sanctioned by your parents should have been sufficient for him to merit your eternal dislike. But it did not work out like that. You loved Benny. He wore his accomplishments lightly, his academic prowess, his medals won in chess tournaments, his skill on the violin. He was a modest shy boy, who envied you your ease in female company, your tough-Jew willingness to go into dangerous neighbourhoods with a bicycle chain draped around your shoulders.

You and Benny shared a secret devotion. Moscow was where life was going to begin. Even though, admittedly, neither of you had ever performed a moment of manual labour, you yearned to be part of the workers' paradise. You and Benny had graduated from your Marxist-Zionist youth group, and now attended the same communist cell, which was in a small apartment on Dzielna Street, the home of a sickly schoolmaster, whose daughter brought in tea and cakes for the conspirators. Both you and Benny admired the daughter, who had blonde hair and wise tentative eyes; and for once you did not take the lead. You wanted Benny to have the girl, and you made intercessions on your friend's behalf. After a meeting one night, when the discussion had been about the advisability of socialism in one country, about wise Koba Joe Stalin, about the lives in the sun that Walecki (aka Horwitz) and Jasieński (aka Zysman) and Unszlicht were leading, without word back home, Izio Ludwig (Lewissohn) stood on the stairs with the schoolmaster's daughter. She had modern ideas and did not hear him out as he pleaded Benny's case. She listened at the beginning, arms behind her back, nodding, eyes downcast, until the last members of the cell had left the apartment building. And then she reached for him, put her arms around his neck (reddened, rawed from the bicycle chain that he had become accustomed to wear) and kissed him with a vigour that reminded him of his cousin Tosia from more innocent times.

You thought that was the end of your friendship with Benny. You would not have forgiven a friend's treachery in this way. But Benny forgave you. Benny believed in friendship and loyalty, and anyway he had not expected an answering desire from the schoolmaster's daughter.

'There he is!' says Jenny De Soto.

Spencer's father is standing near the entrance to the casino showroom, inspecting a fountain that tumbles down one blue-lit wall. Jimmy Ludwig has always had an affinity for machinery. He will examine the workings of any mechanism new to him until he has figured out how it works, and then he will pronounce his decision, his disapproval or respect at the maker's work.

'That's very smart,' his father says.

'We've been looking for you,' Spencer says.

Could he be dressed up as a Palestinian, an African boy?—but it does not quite work, it is a presumption to Africa now, as well as to Poland of 1939, to invent Izio Ludwig into another time. We can hardly believe in such obvious lies as universal truth or the human condition.

Spencer retrieves his father and they sit, he and his small retinue, in the second-floor bar of the Horseshoe. It is being colonised now by the film festival. There are others in the black festival T-shirt, travelling strangers who look pompous and bemused, who can only be film-makers.

Spencer, his father and his fan sit at a small round table and Spencer leads his father through stories of his past for the benefit of Jenny De Soto.

'And what about those men?' Spencer asks.

'Which men?'

'Zysman. Walecki. Who were they?'

'They were dead.'

Said so simply, as if this is the natural state of men.

'Executed. They were. Burned.'

'Burned? You mean cremated?'

'Not burned. Burned. Show trials. Burned.'

'Oh, you mean purged?'

'That's right. They were burned.'

And the sickly schoolmaster would soon be dead, along with the rest of that communist cell that had built their dreams of the promised land. It was not just gangs of Polish youths you had to worry about now. The Germans were in town, and eager young Poles would stand beside German soldiers on the entrances to street squares and point out Jews to them. Work gangs were being sent out to clear the swamplands outside of the city, and the Germans saw this as a useful occupation for the Jews of Warsaw, and even if you didn't look especially Jewish a keen-eyed Polish boy would quickly work out your provenance from your street address, the school you went to.

So Benny and you decided to get away. If ever there was a time to enter the promised land, that time was now. So across you went. You and Benny left Warsaw at night, your overcoat heavy with the gold coins that your mother had sewn into the lining. You took the train to Chelm, and spent the first of your gold coins bribing the mayor of a small town to pay for your transit by rowing boat across the Bug into the Ukraine. And how Benny was impressed at your worldly ways, the quiet word, the palmed coin, but then it became an ordeal, the long hike towards Białystok, which was surrounded by pine woods, in which you and Benny, like children in a fairy tale, walked around, lost, forlorn, starting at sudden wildlife noises. Owls in high reaches of the trees, the scrabbling of burrowing foraging animals. You were city boys, this was not your world, navigating your path by starlight through the woods was not what Warsaw had prepared you for.

And this was not so bad. And sleeping on the floor of a kitchen in Białystok, having persuaded the landlady that not all Warsovians were thieves, was not so bad. And finding lice on your body for the first time was not so bad. And going into the Ural mountains to work in a magnesium complex would not have been so bad, if it were not that Benny was not permitted to go with you. You hated the work there, and the loneliness, made all the worse because Benny came to see you but was ordered to leave within twenty-four hours and you never saw him again.

You were one of thousands of Polish refugees there in the Urals, and surely whatever was happening back home was preferable to this. You would be going back home, and you were losing your faith in the USSR, but you still wanted to make it to Moscow in time for the May Day celebrations. You got there too late, by several months, and you were arrested four times in those two days. Wearing your best suit from Warsaw, you did not fit in.

'I stuck out like a sore thumb,' Jimmy Ludwig says.

'A couple of months later he was in Siberia,' Spencer says.

Spencer relates a story that his father had told. After release from Siberia, after finding his way to Totskoye to join up with the Anders Army, after the march down from Tashkent to Iran, his father was close to death again. His body was collapsing from malnutrition and dysentery. The marchers—they were not soldiers yet, and some of them never would be—made camp outside Mashhad. Spencer's father was nearly nineteen years old. He sat in the sun. He never told Spencer where the dozen hard-boiled eggs came from, but this is the scene, maybe the only scene, that Spencer would film from the past. Perhaps he had been told to distribute them to some others around him. Probably he stole them. However he came by them, he sat on the earth beside a tree with his twelve hard-boiled eggs a little away from the camp.

He ate the first one, and then the second. This was the rest of his life. Forcing himself to eat one dozen eggs. And when it was over, when, somehow, magically, he had eaten the entire batch, he vomited and lay down on the earth, to die.

Spencer can visualise the scene. His father lying on his side, perhaps a scatter of broken eggshells surrounding him, the colour of his vomit in the winter Persian sun. He was probably then almost as skinny as he is now. He closes his eyes. He shivers, his arms clutching his sides.

He does not die. The camera holds on the sleeping man, the movements of his mouth, his hand sometimes rising to brush flies away as he sleeps. A soft hubbub of Polish words from the distance, perhaps an argument threatens to flare up and then dies down again. And then little jump-cuts through time, the light darkens, his head is in a slightly different position each time; and it is morning and Izio Ludwig wakes up healed.

And what are the odds on this? That a man should survive Warsaw, Siberia, Monte Cassino? What are the odds that Jimmy Ludwig should be sitting shivering in an Atlantic City bar in 2008?

Chapter Seven

EXT. ATLANTIC CITY BOARDWALK—DAY

SPENCER LUDWIG stands on the beach. JIMMY LUDWIG sits huddled in an electric wheelchair.

SPENCER turns and walks back towards his father. JIMMY presses a button and whizzes forward, just before his son gets to him.

> JIMMY LUDWIG
> Move it, Charlie.

Again, SPENCER is about to reach his father, when JIMMY again goes forward.

SPENCER stands. He lifts his arms and lets them fall again.

In the sky, SEAGULLS swoop and caw and rise.

Extreme close-up: JIMMY LUDWIG'S face, gleeful.

SPENCER takes a step forward. JIMMY spurts forward again. SPENCER stops. JIMMY stops.

INT. ATLANTIC CITY CASINO—DAY

JIMMY LUDWIG and SPENCER LUDWIG sit facing each other at a bar table. The table has an electronic blackjack game built into it, which is obscured by the backgammon set they are playing on.

INT. ATLANTIC CITY HOTEL—DAY

Elevator doors open. Little bit of comic business as JIMMY LUDWIG can't quite steer his wheelchair into the elevator car: he collides with the sides of the door, a metal ashtray fitting on the wall, a passenger waiting to enter.

INT. ATLANTIC CITY HOTEL ROOM—DAY

SPENCER LUDWIG, eyes closed, throws himself on to the bed. JIMMY LUDWIG goes at top speed to the window, knocking over a chair along the way. He rests his elbows on the table and opens the backgammon set.

JIMMY LUDWIG
Let's get to work.

Spencer picks up the telephone. His father disapproves. Spencer has postponed their backgammon game for this.

'Why do you use that, that citation? It's a clip joint.'

'I've got to call Mary.'

'Who?'

'Mary. My daughter. Your granddaughter. It's her birthday, she'd never forgive me if I didn't call.'

He does not tell his father that he has also used this phone to arrange for flowers to be delivered to her. (Florists, no less than hotel telephones, are a racket, a clip joint.) Mary thanks him for the flowers. She says they made her feel like a movie star.

'I want to come live with you,' she says.

'Oh baby.'

She puts her case as being a matter of love. He makes objections and she knocks them down.

'I'm in America, honey.'

'I *love* America. You remember what I said the time you took me to New York?'

'Of course I do. You got out of the taxi and said, *And now my life begins.*'

'I want to live in New York.'

'And you will one day. But anyway, I'm not in New York. I'm in Atlantic City.'

'I'd like that too.'

'I doubt that, but maybe. But I'm coming back to London soon.'

'*You see?!* And then I can come live with you.'

'You know my flat. There's not a lot of room there.'

'I'm small. I don't take up much room.'

That is sort of true, but Mary, although indeed small for her age, manages to fill any space she finds herself in, with her voice and appetites and implements.

'I don't think I'd be that good at looking after you.'

'We'd look after each other. It'll be fun.'

'Yes. Well. It could be.'

'We'd go out for pizza lots of the time and do the fun things that we like to do with each other. And we can watch all the movies you want to show me. I promise I'll watch them quietly, even the Jack Ford ones.'

'John Ford.'

'That's what I said.'

'And what about work and school?'

'I don't go to work.'

'No, but I do.'

'That's OK. I'll do the sorts of things that I should do. Like tidying up, and my homework. I told you, we'll look after each other.'

'It sounds very nice.'

'It will be. It will be very nice. It will be *so* nice.'

'And what about your mother?'

'We don't want *her* with us. That'll spoil everything.'

'Is there a problem?'

'What do you mean?'

'At home? Has something happened?'

'Of course not. It's just so *boring* here.'

'It'd be even more boring with me.'

'Oh that's not true, I know it isn't. We have fun.'

Even when she was a baby, Spencer working upstairs would not be able to resist the lure of Mary. A few months old, Mary had a sense of humour. The sight of her always made Spencer's heart lift. A script abandoned upstairs, Spencer would sit with his daughter on the living-room floor and they would play with plastic teacups or unpleasant miniature farm animals and make each other laugh.

'You don't make me eat Brussels sprouts.'

'No, that's true, I don't,' he concedes.

'And you wouldn't make me eat Brussels sprouts. *You* don't eat Brussels sprouts.'

'No. They're horrible. Mean and bitter.'

'That's what I think too. And you might let me get my ears pierced.'

'Might I?'

'Yes. I think you might. *And* you let me watch TV on a school night. Not like—'

'Not like who?'

'Nobody. I was just saying.'

'Oh. OK.'

'I'm not talking about anything in true life. It's just suppose.'

'Yes. Of course. I know that. But look, honey. I should go.

Do you want to say hello to Papa Jimmy? I think he wants to wish you happy birthday.'

'I suppose so. But promise you'll think about what I said.'

'I promise.'

'And you mustn't tell anyone what we're planning.'

'We're not planning anything. All I said was I'll think about it.'

'You know what I mean. Just like our secret.'

'Sure. Our secret. I better go. I love you.'

'I love you too, Daddy.'

'Here's Papa Jimmy.'

Grandfather and granddaughter are equally reluctant conversationalists. Neither can ever really understand what the other is saying. And how Spencer cringes when he hears his father bravely trying to wish Mary a happy birthday and say, *Happy New Year!* in the saddest of jaunty ways.

Returning to the endless backgammon game, Spencer manages to explain to his father about his daughter's plan. His father is quick with his opinion.

'Just say yes, she'll forget about it.'

He had thought he had gone beyond being shocked by anything of his father's. Is this the substance of the Jimmy Ludwig doctrine of childcare? Might it even be true? Maybe that was why he had learned never to ask anything of his father.

When the telephone rings, his father waves an unsteady hand towards it.

'Spencer,' his father says.

The saying of his name by his father gives Spencer a gentle pleasure. He nods. He does not answer the phone. He expects it to be his stepmother, or his daughter, or his producer, one of the women in his life who want something from him or, worse, want to give him something.

Spencer's father won't answer the phone either, but the fact that Spencer won't do it agitates him. He puffs out his cheeks and blows and painfully shakes his head at his son.

'Look. If you want to speak to her, you can always call her,' Spencer says.

His father does not answer. He rolls his dice and picks off one of Spencer's pieces and slams it down on the bar.

'What's going to happen if *she* dies before you?' Spencer asks.

He has tried this topic before, to push his father's mind into the future, into making some plan for himself. He has tried to contemplate the ménage that might result, three generations of Ludwig squeezed into Spencer's flat, but the prospect is more or less unthinkable.

'Then you'll be loaded.'

'That's not really what I meant. I'm trying to get you to think about your situation. You must have thought about it, talked about it. What happens if you die first?'

'Then she'll be loaded!'

His father is triumphant in his logic. And is this what it's all about, this good-son business? If his father were poor, would Spencer be so assiduous in his care? He has avoided thinking about it. He usually tries, in his own way, to be honest.

'OK. What about your funeral? Have you made plans for your funeral?'

'Don't worry. It's taken care of.'

'Really? Everything? The form of it, how you want the service to be. Have you chosen music?'

Spencer has chosen the music for his own funeral. A recording of the Kaddish, as performed by Clara Rockmore on the theremin, to be followed by Townes Van Zandt's 'You Are Not Needed Now', played live by his friends Charlie and Mathew and Robert, on vocals, drums and piano. He is not sure he wants Charlie to be the singer. It is probable that Robert will predecease him. This is how rich men must think. They tamper around with their wills; Spencer changes the members of his funeral band. Sometimes Rick Violet is the singer, usually he isn't.

'It's paid for.'

'That's not what I meant.'

He has become accustomed to thinking his thoughts out loud, to carry on a kind of interior monologue, bouncing his words off the uncomprehending eyes of his father.

'I'm not dead yet,' his father says.

'I know you're not,' Spencer says in an effort of conciliation.

'And when I am, what do I care?'

'I don't know. I really don't know.'

There is a sort of crack in Spencer's soul that corresponds, he believes, almost to the shape of his father.

'How much?'

'How much what?' Spencer says.

'How much do you need?'

'I don't know.'

'Yes you do.'

His father understands him this well at least, that Spencer knows exactly how much money he owes in the world, to the bank, to the credit card company, to his ex-nearly-wife, and, most irksomely, to Michelle, who is the only one on the list that he likes. Like Mary's when she arrived in New York, his life can only begin when he cuts free from all his obligations, when he pays Michelle what he owes her.

Spencer's father gets up from the table. He goes to the wardrobe, the bathroom, the bedside table.

'What are you doing?'

'Looking for. Citation.'

'Chequebook?'

'Yes. Citation.'

'What for?'

'To pay you. So you can start.'

'That's very kind.'

'Not kind. What do I care?'

That's a good question, and one that Spencer does not want to investigate the answer to.

'I won't take it.'

'You will.'

Spencer will not. He does not want to erase current dependencies with another, more burdensome one.

'No. I won't.'

'You're crazy.'

'Maybe so.'

'You'll take it after I'm dead.'

'That's different.'

'How?'

Another good question, which Spencer can't begin to answer. Why should it make a difference that he receives money from his father while he's alive? Why should that be worse than receiving cash from a dead man? He has the urge to call Michelle, to tell her that he wants to raise money for a project to be called *The Trouble with Money*. But he can't call Michelle, not until he has £27,000 to pay her off with, and the money may not come from his father.

Spencer makes his way downstairs to the film festival floor. Spencer had once made a film—he was between projects, trying to raise money, to force his way back into the productive world—that was a montage of film editing clichés. He had five actors committed to the next, penniless project and he needed to keep them, and himself, busy if he wasn't to lose them along with something else more important and more intangible. A door opens, a match flares, a train goes through a tunnel, an aeroplane takes off from a foggy runway, a woman smiles, a gate slams shut, a conversation between two men cuts between them, jumping into tighter close-up each time, a baby in a pram jolts downstairs—cut quickly to all the menace of the world: baby carriage—wild bear—baby carriage—men with guns—baby carriage—a whirling tornado—baby carriage— earthquake—baby carriage—mushroom cloud of a nuclear storm—baby carriage—psycho with noose approaching—baby carriage nearly at the foot of the stairs now—onrush of car, headlights and horn sounding—carriage one step from foot of stairs—and a woman wakes up in bed screaming. The torturer's steel, the martyr's face. A clock ticks, a man looks at his watch, the surgeon's scalpel lifts, the front legs of an abattoir cow give way, it sinks to its belly, blood spurting from the wound in its throat. An adolescent boy's frantic stare, the cleavage of a beautiful mature woman, the long line of cows in a milking parlour, line of milk cartons in a supermarket, exterior of a desolate corner store with the sign on the window *Closing Down*, a sad man walks into a dingy back room, a revolver waiting on a plain wooden table, two youths run through a field, clouds in a murky sky, rain splashes on to the surface of a river, a hand turns a tap, a pretty girl lifts a glass of water to her mouth. A door opens. A match flares.

It was all done with style and attention to detail, entirely straight-faced and deadpan; the humour was in the material, not in the makers' attitude to it. Every scene, every costume, each tip of an actor's hat was as authentic as Spencer could make it. And maybe that was why it was so successful with its audience, or maybe it was because it was done so quickly, a *jeu d'esprit. These are films for throwing away,* Fassbinder once said, and *One Door Opens* was Spencer Ludwig's own thrown-away film.

It attracted a following, it spawned its imitators, it became its own cliché. Spencer didn't care, it was his thrown-away film; the fact that it had a life was none of his concern.

Spencer walks down the corridor to the film festival viewing room. The area is not as crowded as a Featured Director might wish. Spencer walks modestly, his laminated badge (*Spence Lunwig, Featured Director*) swinging against his new black T-shirt, from which the logo and lettering have yet to fade. A young man dressed in the black livery of the festival sits on a stool outside the viewing room with his attention on the laptop on his lap. Spencer shows his name badge but the young man does not shift his gaze. Going past, Spencer looks back to see the poker game on the young man's screen.

Spencer Ludwig's retrospective is not what he had expected it to be. In the beige-and-tan room, with immovable windows looking out on to the Wild West casino, are eight television monitors. Beside each, pinned to the wall like labels in an art gallery, are lists of the films showing upon them. There are three presumptive cinéastes in the room, who are doing a slow bored tour of the monitors. Spencer identifies the screen showing his own films. It is the climactic scene of *Robert W's Last Walk*, his favourite of his own films, which happens, co-incidentally or not, to be the one that attracted no foreign sales, for either film or television, and had only a brief first run, hardly any repertory showings, and appeared once on British television, only, it seemed, to demonstrate just how precise the instruments had become that registered how low audience figures could go. Spencer had employed as the lead an old character actor, who could turn in the most accomplished performance on the first take, but whose alcohol dependency meant that each subsequent take got worse and worse. They shot the picture in an old Austrian village outside Vienna, where the actor (who had once been a leading Beckett inter-preter, but whose almost-familiarity came from his work in 1970s sitcoms, 1980s soap operas and 1990s television commercials) developed a liking for schnapps.

Spencer's attention, which has been wandering to the custo-dian's laptop (he is playing a multi-table Hold 'Em tournament as well as grinding away at a one dollar-two dollar Omaha game), is fixed by the final image of the title character, who has turned away once again from the camera (it is one of the strategies of the movie that the title character is always resisting the camera's gaze, always trying to find some modest private place, with the implication, never brazenly stated, that the camera and the audience might well be improved by learning a little tact), and makes the timidly grand gesture of lifting his hands away from his sides and touching his thumbs together.

Spencer is always moved by this moment. The film, as if, finally, belatedly, learning to respect Robert W's privacy, fades slowly to black, with Robert W's hands the last part of the image to disappear. There are no end credits. The moment of aloneness is meant to be shared by the cinema audience. But there is hardly any audience in this room. And neither does the moment of darkness, of aftermath (which, obscurely, Spencer personifies as female), sustain as she is meant to because the films are on some automatic DVD loader—and immediately *One Door Opens* loads with its first shot of a door opening.

'Look,' says a chubby man in shorts, whose attention has been taken by Spencer's work at last. 'That's like the commercial. The one for that cereal.'

'Oh yeah, it's really annoying,' says his companion.

Spencer has given no permission for his film to be used for a commercial for cereal or indeed any other product. This is against his narrow set of principles. He is not surprised or even dismayed. Something he cannot quite identify has been confirmed.

Chapter Eight

Spencer is in danger of confusing genres. This is not a scene from an independent film, it's rebel Hollywood from the early 1970s, Michael Sarrazin and an ironically resurrected tough guy from a darker, more uncomplicated era—Sterling Hayden maybe, or Robert Ryan, Lawrence Tierney, even Elisha Cook Jr, if we are going down the ultra-ironic route—meet Karen Black and Carol Kane, a glimpse of the sea, another way of living, two girls of easy virtue and kind ways and only half-surrendered hopes, the four of them discovering an unlikely respite of shared humanity and heart. But everything is against them—the Corporation, the war in Vietnam, the past, men in ties and houndstooth jackets—and the world will explode in a Technicolor® starburst (with cinematography by Vilmos Zsigmond).

Drussilla is from Latvia, Tanya says she is American. Her accent though is rough with unfamiliar edges and utterly unplaceable to Spencer.

'Where are you from?' he asks.

'Wherever you want me to be from, honey,' she says.

'I don't really have a preference. I was just interested,' he says.

Tonight is the gala and Spencer is nervous. He has his tuxedo ready, the one his father gave him several years before, a relic from the early 1970s, wide lapel, discreet flare. He has ironed the faded black T-shirt (*Vive le Rock!*) that he will wear underneath. And then he was sitting staring at his father and his father was sitting staring at him, and time was dripping far too slowly around them, until his father suggested they go to the bar for a drink. Which is where they met Drussilla and Tanya, or, rather, Drussilla and Tanya met them, attracted perhaps by the heavy gold band that Spencer, its unlikely owner, wears clasped around his left wrist.

Both Drussilla and Tanya wear high-heeled shoes, short skirts, tight blouses. Drussilla's hair is frosted blonde, piled up on her head in a tumble of curls that her slender neck looks unready to support. Tanya's hair is long and sleek and dark, falling almost to the small of her back.

Spencer's father breathes harder. Long ago, Spencer's father took Spencer's stepbrothers to Kennedy Airport, where he taught them techniques in how to pick up air stewardesses. When Spencer had heard about this, he was tearfully jealous. Spencer was only twelve at the time, but he was thirsty for experience, particularly shared experience with his father.

'My father,' Spencer announces to Tanya and Drussilla, 'taught me how to fold up a T-shirt.'

'Is that right?' Drussilla says, scratching her naked thigh, which is smeared in make-up that colours it brown. Spencer wonders whether there are bruises hidden there. For the first time in this encounter, he experiences a small pang of erotic feeling.

'Yes,' Spencer says. 'And how to roll up a rope. And a hose. Hosepipe. That's it, I think. That's what I learned from my father.'

'Your son is angry at you,' Drussilla says.

'Angry, I don't know. Resentful maybe. Other fathers teach

their sons stuff. Constellations, the names of stars. How to fix a motorbike or pick up stewardesses at Kennedy Airport. I can fold up a T-shirt. Oh. And a towel. He also showed me how to fold a towel. It's the same sort of principle, you do it in sections, thirds. I think he learnt it in the army.'

'I won't tell you what my father taught me,' Tanya says, and she and Drussilla laugh hard and heartily.

The bar they are sitting in has no windows. Its walls are beige and cream, with prints of Venetian canals and posters advertising ice cream and sunglasses. A barman stands, looking as bored as Drussilla and Tanya, polishing glasses. Three men play video slot machines embedded into the bar counter. A woman, dressed similarly to Drussilla and Tanya, teeters on a stool.

And Spencer's father sits with his glass of water in front of him in which the ice slowly melts. Is he enjoying this? Does he have any capacity left for sexual desire or feeling? Do these women signify erotic possibility to him?

'How are you doing?' Spencer says to him.

'A million bucks,' says Spencer's father, who reaches an unsteady hand towards Tanya's hair. 'What is this?'

'Dad!' Spencer says. 'I'm sorry. He's a little old and rickety.'

'What is rickety?' Drussilla says.

'I don't know. Sort of ramshackle and falling apart.'

'Ramshack?'

'Yes. I know. I'm sorry. It's amazing how many words we use that have all sorts of metaphorical meanings. Ramshackle. I suppose it means about to fall down. But I guess rickety must come from rickets. It's a disease. Poor children used to get it. I think it's a vitamin deficiency of some kind.'

'Your father has disease?'

'Many. But not like that.'

'Like what?'

Spencer's father continues to stroke Tanya's hair in a marvelling kind of way.

'He's a live one,' Tanya says.

'What is this?' he repeats.

'I'm sorry,' Spencer says again.

'It's OK, I like it,' Tanya says. She raises her voice to answer Spencer's father. 'It's hair. Human hair.'

'But not yours,' Spencer's father says.

'Well it is mine. I paid top dollar for it.'

'Exactly,' Spencer's father says.

'I'm sorry,' Spencer says. 'With age he's becoming a little, disinhibited.'

'What about your teeth? Are they yours?' Tanya says.

'Absolutely.'

'Did you grow them yourself?'

'Touché,' Spencer's father says and, rather rakishly, tips the glass of iced water to his bloodless lips in the same way that, Spencer decides, he would have sipped a vodka gimlet in a long-ago JFK bar in the company of his stepsons and two or three stewardesses fresh in the glamour of the golden age of jet travel.

Spencer is drunk. He is also, he realises, smiling. He hugs his father, whose bones are cold and dry beneath his touch, and his father hugs back, and his strength, or some of it, is still there.

'I've got to call Mary,' Spencer says.

'Who's Mary?' someone says.

'Got to call my daughter.'

'How old is she?'

'Ten. She's ten. Got to call her.'

'That's a great age, a terrific age. I used to be ten,' the barman says.

'Shall I dance for you?' Jimmy Ludwig says. He pushes up from the wheelchair and totters, like a toddler taking tentative balance, or a retired boxer finding his feet on returning to the ring.

Spencer's father had performed this routine when Spencer

was young. 'Shall I dance for you?' he would say, and step into the moves he must have learned from the cinema, Sammy Davis Jr, maybe, a Sinatra rat-pack film, shoulders hunched, arms tight to the sides, small jive steps, eyes downcast, mouth a little open, hands gently rubbing the air in front of his chest. And Spencer would always say, *Yes, yes, go on*, but his father would always stop, the ironic gesture of promise would be over (*the things we could do, if only we believed in them!*) and, slightly more relaxed than before, he would resume whatever his inter-rupted occupation had been.

'No, it's OK, I think we ought to be getting on,' Spencer says. 'What time is it?'

'Look at your subpoena.'

'Oh.'

'That's a pretty watch,' Drussilla says, leaning closer to him.

'Patek Philippe,' his father says.

'No, it's Piaget,' Drussilla says.

'That's right,' Jimmy Ludwig says.

'Maybe we ought to be getting ready—the gala,' Spencer says.

Spencer's father gets to his feet. Spencer, slightly surprised, thinks this is in dutiful response, but then realises by the panicky look in his father's eyes that he needs the bathroom.

'Can we come?' Tanya says.

These girls don't know the workings of Jimmy Ludwig's bladder the way his son does.

'He's just going to the men's room,' Spencer says.

Spencer gets up too, to offer his arm and support, but his father shakes him off and makes his dangerous journey across the barroom on his own, tugging his oxygen tank on the wheels that Dwight thoughtfully has provided.

'To the gala,' Tanya says.

'Oh.'

If this were an independent film, then that is exactly what

should happen, the drunk film-maker and his decaying father in the company of two bewigged prostitutes who smell of hair-spray and perfume and champagne tottering into the gala dinner, adding some death and sin to the room, lifting the inevitable boredom of film professionals, the local dignitaries, the critics for the *Paterson Bugle*, the *Summit Times*, the *Ventnor Gazette*, and all the hangers-on and apparatchiks who make a living out of the creativity and self-doubt of others.

'He's a very sweet man,' Drussilla says.

'Who is?' Spencer says.

'Your father.'

'Is he? No. Not really. Sweet I don't think really describes him.'

In the car, Spencer had asked his father whether there were any compensations of old age. His father had said there was none, but here was one at least, albeit of indeterminate value, the sweet impression made upon the perceptions of Latvian hookers.

'I've never heard anyone describe him as sweet before,' Spencer says. 'When I was a child he had this thing he used to say, *Nobody's perfect. Except for me, of course.*'

'You say you're perfect?' Drussilla says with some surprise.

'No. Not me. Nobody is. It's not possible. He just used to say that he was. It was a joke but I think he really sort of meant it.'

'You shouldn't pick on him,' Tanya says.

'I'm not picking on him.'

'He's an old man.'

'I know he is.'

'He's sick.'

'Tell me about it. I have a list up in our room of all his conditions and all his medications.'

'You're a good son,' Drussilla says, abruptly changing tack. Maybe a look had slipped between the women encouraging each other to go easy on Spencer, in the interests of future profit, or maybe some virtue of his was finally shining out.

'Thank you,' Spencer says. 'I don't know. Sometimes I wonder, you know, why.'

'Why what?' Drussilla says.

'Why I do this. I live in London. I have a life there, of some sort, and my father was a terrible father to me, when I was a child.'

'So why are you here?'

'Well this time, it's clear. I was invited. The festival, the gala. I'm a film-maker.'

'That's cool,' Drussilla says.

'But I mean in general. Spending time in the States, sacrificing my time and so forth.'

'Is your father rich?' Tanya says. 'Maybe he's going to leave you a lot of his money in his will.'

'I've thought about that. I mean, no,' (and hurriedly he rolls his jacket sleeve down over the watch) 'he isn't rich. But yes, he probably will leave me something, he's got some money. But I've wondered about my motivation. I wonder if there's a part of me that's just bent on guarding my inheritance.'

'You're a good person,' Drussilla says, leaning in closer and stroking his arm in a way that he can't quite decide is pleasurable or in fact rather irritating.

'I don't know. I've never thought of myself as a particularly good person. But there's something that feels good about doing the right thing, you know what I'm saying? Doing your duty, performing loving acts. Maybe that's why nurses can put up with all the things they have to put up with. I'm sure the good ones have a vocation.'

'I used to be a nurse. I hated it,' Tanya says.

'I'm sure I would too. But life is complicated, most of the time we don't know what the right thing to do is, and then occasionally, very occasionally, it's clear. You do know what it is, and then it isn't so hard to do it. I think I want another drink. Does anyone want another drink? But there's another thing.

When I was young, my father frightened me more than anyone. A harsh word from him would make me cry, instantly. I don't think I've ever told anyone that. He was the smartest and toughest man I had ever met and he had no idea or even interest, I suppose, in what went on inside my head, and he exerted this unreasonable power over me.'

'I don't know if I understand what you are saying but for sure I think you're a good son and a good person,' Drussilla says.

'Thank you,' Spencer says. 'I don't think you're right but I appreciate you saying that.'

'Maybe you've forgiven him. Or maybe you're trying to forgive him,' Tanya says.

'I don't think so. We're not Christians.'

Spencer wonders if that is the point of this enterprise, and all his others, to work against sickly notions of redemption and Christian love.

'I think what I might be doing now is just following things through to the end,' Spencer says.

'Where *is* your father?' Tanya says.

'Oh. He's been a while, hasn't he? I'd better check.'

Spencer walks through the dismal bar. The door to the men's room does not properly open. He tries it two, three times, but blocking it is some impediment, an obstacle, soft yet unyielding, that Spencer thuds the door against, and which, Spencer realises, when he gets cumbersomely down to his knees and cranes his neck around the part-opened door, is his father's head.

Tanya, with dampened wads of toilet paper, dabs the blood away from Spencer's father's forehead and scalp.

'I'm sorry,' Spencer says.

His father just stares at him.

If this were a Hollywood film, or the sort of independent film that captures an international audience, it would turn into heart-break now, decorous hospital decline, the truths made manifest, we are all children destined to be orphaned, how do we choose to meet our deaths, how can we bear to be bystanders to anyone else's?—Or else it would abruptly lift into a caper now, Spencer and his father against the casino, father's wisdom, son's audacity, fanciful music swirling around them, the percussion of chips, the crowd of tourists huddling in, clapping hands in delight, his father with bandaged head breaking the bank, consternation on the faces of the pit bosses, who look up in bafflement at the ceiling cameras and whisper to croupiers to change the cards, the dice, as the long-buried plan that his father had cooked up years ago is disinterred and magically flourishes. The thrilled crowd gets larger, and nothing can stop them, high-fives behind Spencer and his father, who wear their Playboy mansion tuxedos, bottles of champagne, casino lights, the towers of chips build and scatter around them, and all the slot machines release their load in a singing siren of jangly bells and electronic mating calls.

But this is not a Hollywood film or an independent that calculates its way into the box-office top ten, or even one of Spencer's that he can exert some slow control over. He is in a hotel room in Atlantic City and his damaged father lies bleeding on the bed and one prostitute cleans up his wounds and the other is on the phone ordering room service.

'He must have fallen,' Tanya says.

'Yes, I worked that one out,' Spencer says.

'You do not have to be rude.'

'I'm sorry,' Spencer says.

'What dressing does everybody want on their salad?' Drussilla says.

'Gala,' says Spencer.

'They have ranch dressing, blue cheese, French, Russian, oil and vinegar.'

'Party. It's time for the party.'

'We can look after him, you go to your gala. Can we order room service, please?'

'There'll be food there.'

'I didn't think you wanted us to come.'

'Please. Be my guests.'

And Spencer is suddenly worried. Not at what his hosts from the festival, Mike and Cheryl Baumbach and their people, might say or think, the gesture of arriving at a film festival gala in the company of two hookers, but he has, he realises, been thinking of this all as the film he is making, and he is worried. The *mise-en-scène* is fine. In fact, as some of his more formalist critics like to point out, the look of his films is hardly their strongest point. A splash of colour to register an emotion is as strenuous as he will usually go—Spencer has always approved of accidental beauty, the chanceful moment, the way the unexpected light captures an actor's eyes, a crumpled drinks carton forgotten in a corner of the set becomes a perfect object, poignant with meaning. It's going to look right, the casino is perfect, the Boardwalk a place of irony and charm, where the seen merges with the previously unimagined, where the already apprehended twists in on itself and casts everything into a new light; but the project is beginning to open itself up to some unsavoury interpretations. This prostitution storyline is not one he would have chosen.

'What will the feminists think? What will the critics say?' Spencer says.

'Since when has that bothered you?' his father says quite succinctly.

'Everything bothers me,' Spencer says. 'Every unkind word. The fall of every bird in God's creation.'

'Fancy talk to impress the ladies,' his father says.

Spencer struggles out of his jeans. Drussilla raises an eyebrow.

'Not sure if that's appropriate right now, honey. But hey,' Tanya says.

'No. Let's get going.'

He manages, in drunkenness, in grandeur, to climb into his tuxedo, which is somewhat tighter in the waist than it used to be.

Nurse Tanya is not convinced that Jimmy Ludwig should go to a party. She thinks he should rest.

'For what?' Spencer says.

He had anticipated difficulty in smuggling in his extra guests, but the ballroom is barely two-thirds full. Spencer is placed at the table of New Jersey film-makers. Drussilla and Tanya are banished to a far corner of the room, while his father sits with film-makers' husbands, wives and partners. This is the sort of thing his father detests above all, to be in public, with people he does not know, swimming hopelessly in the cross-currents of words that sound like a foreign language to him. He never liked social occasions at the best of times, of which this is not one. On Spencer's left is Ron, a director of wildlife documentaries; on his right is Suzie, who makes lesbian horror films.

Spencer keeps looking around to check on his father, who, nonetheless, is making a brave stab at acting the part of a party guest who is enjoying himself. Spencer's father has always had a beautiful smile, which Spencer suspects is a trick of facial muscles rather than a revelation of the soul.

'Don't you?'

Something is being asked of Spencer, who has been hardly paying attention to the conversation at the table.

'Yes, absolutely,' he says.

'What did he say?'

'He said, *Absolutely*.'

He is being discourteous to a group of people whom, he supposes, he could loosely call colleagues. Politely, he throws himself back into the life of the table. Suzie is being quizzed by the man on her right about some of the more technical aspects of her craft, which is presumably code for the questioner's interest in lesbian sex. Spencer turns to Ron.

'Wildlife, eh?'

'That's right,' Ron says.

'Bears?'

'Yes. I have done bears.'

'Aren't you frightened of them?'

'Why should I be?'

'Because they might kill you.'

'Bears are very much misunderstood.'

'Really?'

'They're beautiful creatures.'

'How can they be?'

Spencer mistrusts any manifestation of beauty that is not the human body or man-made. He thinks it sentimental to consider nature beautiful. Spencer believes in the beauty of the nape of a woman's neck, the shape she makes when she lifts her arms to fix her hair, the curve of her thigh. He thinks athletes are beautiful, and tall buildings. Skyscrapers are beautiful in a way that mountains can never be. But Spencer does not want to get into an argument about aesthetics, the beautiful and the sublime.

'Tell me, if I meet a bear, what should I do?'

'Depends what kind of bear.'

'OK. A grizzly. What should I do if a grizzly bear attacks me?'

'Where do you live? Australia? It's not going to happen.'

'Just suppose. What if.'

'OK. Play dead. Curl up in the foetal position with your hands protecting your head like so. But if it's a black bear then make as much noise as you can and they'll probably go away. They eat carrion so if you play dead they'll probably try to eat you. But the best thing is just not to bother them. Most bear attacks are mothers defending their young.'

'Black bear make a lot of noise, grizzly play dead.'

'That's right.'

'What are you two talking about?'

Suzie has managed to elude her interlocutor, who is picking at his shrimp cocktail and rubbing his thigh with his hand.

'Ron is instructing me in the art of survival skills.'

'Spencer is concerned he might get attacked by bear.'

'Me too! Ever since I was a kid.'

'Ron says, if it's a grizzly you should make a lot of noise and that'll probably scare it away. A black bear, then play dead.'

Spencer sees Ron about to correct him and then stop himself. Perhaps Ron wants him, everybody, dead, ripped apart by a grizzly bear, or eaten by a black bear for carrion.

'That's good to know.'

'Are you scared of any other animals?' Spencer asks.

'Most of them,' Suzie says. 'Dogs of course, especially the little yappy ones because they seem to have a kind of Napoleon complex. I don't like cats but that's not because they scare me. Just that I find them a little . . .'

'Creepy?'

'Yes. Exactly.'

'What about cows?'

'I don't really have much feeling either way about cows.'

'I detest them,' Spencer says. 'Not because I'm scared they're going to kill me. Although, if you look at the statistics, the numbers of cow-related deaths are going up exponentially. It's like Ron's bears, they think they're protecting their young so they try to manoeuvre you to the edge of the field, the fence or the hedgerow or something, and then you know what they do? They tip over on to their sides to crush you. Isn't that horrible?'

'Horrible,' says Suzie.

Ron is staring at the two of them in disgust. He has a stringy yellow moustache and loyal blue eyes. He probably does yoga to a very high standard and bakes his own bread and makes extremely long explanations to children.

'Can you imagine it? Can you think of a more horrible way to die? Lying in a field being slowly crushed to death under a cow. But as I say, that's not what really gets me about them. It's their eyes. Have you ever looked into a cow's eyes?'

'I can't say that I have.'

'Ron. Have you ever looked into a cow's eyes?'

Ron makes a non-committal shrug.

'You know what you see there? Nothing. Absolutely nothing. That's what offends me. There's an utter absence of intelligence in their eyes. I find it loathsome.'

'I know what you mean,' Suzie says.

'It's bullshit,' Ron says.

'I like donkeys though. And tortoises,' Spencer says.

'Really?' Suzie says, without enthusiasm or interest.

'Ron bakes his own bread,' Spencer says.

'So do I!' Suzie says. 'Isn't it the best thing?'

Spencer had liked Suzie before. He likes her even better for baking her own bread. He likes Ron too. He admires his outdoor skills, his calmness. Ron could probably build a shack in the woods and survive for years on a diet of berries and his own urine. But he has lost his two table neighbours to each other. They lean forward and then back to find a route past Spencer to talk about gauges of flour and bread recipes, sourdough and pumpernickel.

This is not quite what Spencer had been expecting from the gala dinner. It looks like more fun at the international table, where the real Albanian is giving some kind of lecture, with the help of an interpreter, who, Spencer realises when he looks at her more closely, is the multi-talented Jenny De Soto, dressed for the occasion in a black evening dress that spangles and shimmers in the lights. The real Albanian is a small, clerical-looking man with close-cropped grey hair and a fearsomely intelligent, perhaps slightly feral face. It is well known that he has worked with Tarkovsky and Chris Marker.

Spencer would like to hear the real Albanian's wisdom. He would like to be playing poker. He would like to be feeling even drunker than he already is. He picks up the nearest bottle and splashes more wine into his own glass and into the glasses of the neighbours at his table.

'No thank you,' Ron says.

Cheryl and Mike Baumbach, who look more like sister and brother than wife and husband, take to the podium. A tapping of microphones, a shriek of feedback, sarcastic cheers from the tables.

'Welcome,' says Cheryl Baumbach. 'We're so thrilled that you're here, the creative communities of New Jersey.'

'This is great, it's so great, this is our dream, Cheryl and I,' Mike says. 'Uh, please. Jerry?'

The Baumbachs step away from the podium towards opposite sides and look behind. The ballroom lights dim, an image appears on the screen, the Short Beach Film Festival logo, accompanied by a painfully thunderous slash of organ music that elicits shouts and desperate pleadings from the creative community of New Jersey.

'*Jerry!*' Cheryl Baumbach yells.

The music cuts out and then timidly reappears, growing slowly, to settle at a tolerable volume. And we see shots of the Atlantic City Boardwalk and the sea, black and white, slightly out of focus, a photograph, colour now, of a group of school-children looking inexplicably excited in a classroom, two men, one black, the other Asian, playing chess in a park. And now we see clips of films, which Spencer supposes to be the fruits of the creative community of New Jersey, a montage of two-shots of couples, usually young, usually looking bored, in a bedroom, a bar, sitting in a field, which is followed by a sequence of long-shots of men walking, in city streets, along a beach, a bridge, men in suits carrying briefcases or laptop bags, men in suits carrying nothing at all except for a vague hunted look, men in chinos and T-shirts, men in surfer shorts and T-shirts.

'What's the point of this?' Spencer asks, but neither Suzie nor Ron responds. Suzie is looking sort of dazed. Ron is staring impatiently at the screen, waiting, we suppose, for the montage of wildlife shots, the birds taking flight over the river, the mother bears suckling their young.

'Could we have a word?'

Crouching beside Spencer's chair, knees creaking in unison, are Mike and Cheryl Baumbach.

'It's a great pleasure to be here,' Spencer says.

'And we're ecstatic to have you,' Cheryl says, with equal lack of feeling.

'We have a little problem,' Mike says.

'I'm sorry to hear that. Would you like some wine?' Spencer says.

'It's quite a big problem,' Cheryl says.

'Of a fiduciary nature,' Mike says.

'Mike's put everything into this.'

'It does you credit,' Spencer says.

'It's all gone,' Mike says.

'What is?'

'Everything. Pfft. *Pfft.*'

Mike Baumbach makes little popped-balloon whizzing noises and waves a hand to signify the loss of it all.

'I don't quite get it,' Spencer admits.

'There's a fellow called Dwight. Works at the front desk at the hotel.'

'*Worked*,' corrects Cheryl.

'Worked, works, worked. Used to work at the front desk.'

'Of course, yes. I know Dwight. He's been very helpful.'

'That's kind of the point.'

'A little *too* helpful.'

'I'm sorry. I don't understand.'

'He's bust the bank,' says Mike.

'He had access to the festival account,' says Cheryl.

'Pffft. Pffft. *Pffffft*,' says Mike.

'Took it on himself to . . .'

'Expedite and facilitate?'

'That's what he called it.'

'The weird thing is that he hasn't taken a thing for himself as far as we can tell,' says Cheryl.

'Pffft,' says Mike.

'But you, for example, and your father.'

'That wheelchair, for example.'

'The oxygen equipment.'

'And assorted sundries. We figure about twenty-eight thousand dollars.'

'Blimey. That's a lot.'

'Isn't it.'

'So whenever you get a chance to reimburse us.'

'First available opportunity.'

'That would be great.'

Spencer is having trouble processing this. But a further, more imperative thought pushes everything else away.

'Bollocks,' Spencer says.

About to refill his glass, reaching for the wine bottle across the dark debris of the table, the lights from the promotional film show shining rather prettily through the glasses and bottles and water jug, the realisation hits him that his father has been on the same oxygen cylinder for about four hours. It will be dangerously low now, perhaps even empty.

Spencer gets up so abruptly that his chair topples over on to its back. He does not investigate the ensuing sounds, the muffled thud, crash of glass, a soft dripping of liquid, an outraged Cheryl Baumbach squeak. His way to his father's table is fast but unsteady. His hands come into contact with unexpected surfaces, a vase of flowers, a lighted candle, a bearded gentleman's face, the wet contents of a soup bowl, a woman's left breast.

His father is asleep, mouth open, breath shallow, one end of the tube hanging away from his left nostril, the other still fixed in place.

'Come on, Dad,' Spencer says.

He eases his father's legs over so he is perched on his wheel-chair in an approximate driving position. Jimmy Ludwig mutters angrily in his sleep, jerks his arms away to make a pillow against the seat-rest and shifts further to curl towards a foetal position.

'No. Sorry.'

Spencer forces his father to sit straight in his chair, trying to go gentle with the fragile bones, not to grip too hard on the bruisable skin, and he remembers with some annoyance that his most recent failed New Year's resolution had been never to apologise and only occasionally to explain. Spencer switches on the ignition, and his father flops away again into a position more comfortable for sleep.

'Bollocks,' says Spencer.

'Sssh!' hisses someone near by.

'Sorry,' says Spencer. 'Fuck. Bollocks.'

'*SSSH!*'

On the screen, delighting Ron no doubt, probably even authored by Ron, is a close-up of a pair of white horses in a field. Spencer does not have the time to admire or dread their sleekness or their eyes. He clambers on to the back of the wheel-chair, straddling the engine, as if his father were a motorcycle rider and he the pillion passenger. His father drifts away and then back again, cracking Spencer on the chin with the crown of his head. Spencer leans forward, forcing his father to sit straight, and reaches past him for the handlebars. He presses the machine into gear.

Off they go, tentative at first, nudging against feet, steering into and away from the legs of chairs. He has the choice to proceed like this, inching around the obstacles in the ballroom, human and otherwise, or just to shut his eyes and aim for the most direct path to the door. His father's eyes are, as far as he can tell, still shut, his chin resting on his surgical collar. Spencer twists the handlebar that controls acceleration and off they go, skittering, colliding, raising yelps and sudden accusations, but they keep going, gathering speed, snagging a loose corner of a tablecloth here, ripping a trouser leg there, rolling over electricity cables, fallen wineglasses, pools of grease and meat, plump feet overstuffed into dainty evening slippers.

'Stop that wheelchair!' somebody yells.

The double doors open before them, perhaps out of inanimate terror, and Spencer and his father are blazing a path along the red carpet of a hotel corridor.

A boy, his mouth smeared with chocolate sauce, raises an ice-cream cone towards them in salutation. In the elevator, a prim-looking man riding his own, less deluxe electric wheelchair nods at Spencer and remarks, *It's the only way to travel*, to which Spencer manages to mumble some kind of response.

Spencer's father is alarmingly light. Spencer carries him from his wheelchair and lays him down on the bed. He switches on the oxygen machine and attaches the tube to his father's nose. There is an immediate beneficial effect. His father's chest rises more fully with each breath. His eyes drift open again, slowly focus on Spencer.

'Who?' he says.

'Yes,' Spencer says, terribly and wretchedly sober. 'Don't worry. You're fine.'

The telephone rings. Spencer does not answer it. There is blood again on his father's head. Spencer wipes it away with toilet paper, and more seeps out again. He pulls over the armchair and watches his father, who tugs irritably at the tube in his nose and then lets his hands fall by his sides.

When Spencer lifts a hand to his own face he finds another source for the blood that was on his father's head. It smears on to his fingertips from the cut on his chin.

Spencer watches over his father. The hours go by. His father sleeps unlaboured and peaceful. Spencer puts on his street clothes.

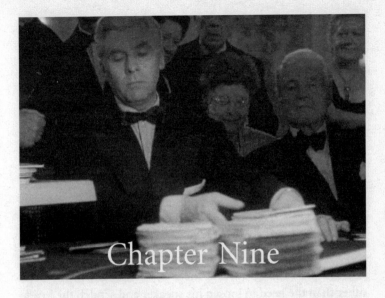

Chapter Nine

He has no destination in mind. Spencer walks through the casino at night, the slot machine players, the last indoor smokers in America, the graveyard shift working the poker room, and the sign for tomorrow's tournament with its $250,000 guaranteed prize pool—and how Spencer would love to play in that, first or second prize would liberate him from all dependencies and most obligations. He dodges a pair of black-T-shirted festival reps walking blearily past the High Roller suite carrying broken wineglasses and tired clipboards. On a chair between palm trees, Drussilla and Tanya are curled together, sleeping.

When Spencer sees the Baumbachs, talking fast into cellphones, he takes an unaccustomed exit, away from the sea, on to Pacific Avenue, the high-end stores that are no less empty at night than they are during the day, someone's fitful dream of Vegas, but no one wants Prada in Atlantic City. He walks past the hospital, a convenience store, and up on to Atlantic Avenue. He is hit by a strange sensation that he interprets at first as indigestion, and then maybe as the shock of internal electricity that presages the arrival of a cataclysmic health issue—Dostoyevsky tells us that in the moment before an epileptic fit he is struck by an intensity and a sharpness that make life worth living. Spencer walks along Atlantic Avenue, where he is not alone, there are prostitutes and beggars and slow-rolling cars, and he realises that what he is experiencing is a furtive feeling of freedom, dimly remembered from when he was seventeen and travelling around the country, or that first day on set shooting his own first film, or the night he left his nearly-wife.

He has no plan, no expectations; as Robert W knew, it is good just to walk, sidewalk, muscles, bones, movement, the world. He is tireless, invigorated, inseparable. He has no intention, just to keep on walking is the good thing, so when he stops outside Atlantic Gold, a twenty-four-hour pawnbroker and cheque-cashing bureau, there is no thought in his head other than the need to loosen his sneaker and scratch the inside of his right ankle.

The window of Atlantic Gold is barred and grilled. Behind the metal Spencer sees bowling trophies, jewellery, watches. He does not intend to go inside. He goes inside.

The shopkeeper is a dapper man who reminds him of Dwight, formerly of the hotel, except this man is white, about twenty years older, and unliveried.

'Good evening, sir.'

An audacious action independent of thought suddenly announces itself through Spencer. His father's cheque is in his hand and he is passing it under the glass that declares itself with a bright gay yellow sticker to be bullet-proof.

'Yes?'

'I'd like to cash this please.'

The man glances at the cheque. He does not consent to touch it.

'That's not going to be possible.'

Refusal always strengthens desire, maybe even inspires it.

Spencer empties his wallet of picture IDs and waves them at the glass.

'Look. What more can you want? This is my passport and this is my driver's licence, this is my membership of BAFTA and here, here,' (he waves his misspelled accreditation from the film festival) 'this is me again. I am who I say I am. And the cheque is good.'

'Uh, sir. Two reasons, sir.'

'Yes?'

'For one, this is a cheque-cashing bureau.'

'And this is a cheque!'

'We cash social security and company cheques. Not personal cheques. That's not what we do.'

'Well isn't it time you moved the rules around a little?'

'We get along with our rules perfectly well. I don't think it would be appropriate to change them now.'

'But isn't life a process of becoming? How can we ever know what we might be if we don't allow for the possibility of change?'

How he wishes Dwight were working here. Dwight would expedite and facilitate. Dwight would grasp the philosophical truth straight away.

'That's an interesting point, sir.'

'Well consider it. I won't rush you. I think you know I'm right.'

'Be that as it may, we find ourselves at my second reason.'

Confident in his ontology, Spencer waits to demolish the clerk's second line of philosophical or procedural fortifications.

'Even if we were disposed to cash this cheque, I say *even if*—'

'I hear you saying it.'

'*Even if*, we wouldn't be able to. But that's a pretty watch you're wearing.'

'Thank you. It was a gift, from my father. But look—'

'Piaget?'

'I think it's Patek Philippe actually. But I don't see why you can't bend the rules. Here's my passport, here's a perfectly legitimate cheque. All I'm asking you to do is—'

'Excuse me. If you read the name on the face here, you'll see that it's a Piaget. Nice little piece. Even if the band is somewhat scratched. Nice piece nonetheless.'

'Thank you. But I'm here about the cheque.'

'Yes, well, again, if you look for the name, you'll see that it's not in order.'

'Of course it is. My father signed it—'

'I have no doubt of that, sir.'

'And made it out to me. Look.'

When Spencer jabs his finger at the payee's name scrawled upon the cheque he realises that he had not looked at it before. In the embarrassment of receiving money from his father, he had checked that the figure and words tallied and then squirrelled it away. Carefully, laboriously, along the dotted line for the payee's name, his father had made the cheque out to himself, *Jimmy Ludwig*.

'But as I say, it's a very nice watch.'

'Yes. Thank you. And I—oh. I see. I think I see.'

'Piaget Polo, circa 1982, I would say.'

'And how much would you say it's worth?'

'That of course is a question of interpretation of the market rather than any intrinsic value, those are the times we live in, I'm sad to say, but I think I can safely offer you two thousand dollars for it.'

'Oh. Wow. Right. I mean, couldn't you make it a little more?'

'Two thousand two hundred.'

'The cheque's no good?'

'The cheque's no good. Unfortunately.'

'Two thousand two hundred?'

'Final offer. It is, I am reluctant to tell you, a buyer's market here.'

He had thought he would give the watch to Mary when she was eighteen. A father's gift, a family treasure.

'Who would you sell it to?'

'I couldn't say. It's a question of luck. Most things are.'

'You have more sellers than buyers here.'

'Exactly.'

'You couldn't make it two and a half?'

'Two-two.'

'Like the ballerina.'

'Aha. Yes. Very good.'

'Or the archbishop.'

'Indeed.'

But the response now is a matter of politeness rather than appreciation or humour. The pawnbroker has given of his time and his care, and all that is left is transaction. He seems like a sensitive man and this is probably no kind of work for a sensitive man. He wipes his glass counter. Beneath it, behind locked security grilles, are the testaments of other people's misfortunes, gold watches and diamond bracelets and cufflinks and necklaces. There's one gold chain with the name Debbie hanging down in red jewels or glass.

Two thousand two hundred is less than he needs, but it is a stake. The rule in poker money management is that you should never commit more than five per cent of your bankroll at any one time. But if he takes this money to a cash game he might be able to spin it up into his entry fee to the poker tournament. Spencer used to consider himself a poker player, he could become one again.

'OK. Let's do it.'

'Very good. There's some paperwork here for us to do and you to sign, merely that you attest that the goods you'll be pledging are yours to dispose of, and this will be your receipt and if you wish to redeem your property then this attests that you agree to the terms.'

'Terms?'

'A sliding scale. Ten per cent interest in the first seven days, a further eight per cent interest after a further fourteen days, five per cent after another thirty days, and so forth.'

'Is that standard?'

'Actually quite generous. You could check the terms of our rivals and competitors and colleagues along the Avenue and you would find that we offer comparatively liberal rates. We see it as being in the nature of our business to encourage repeat trade.'

'That's fine. I trust you.'

'Really? That's heart-warming, if dangerous, but essentially I'm glad.'

EXT. ATLANTIC AVENUE—NIGHT

Sweeping lights, pools of shadow. SPENCER LUDWIG walks briskly, one hand firmly on a rear pocket of his jeans. Cars with tinted windows dawdle past, looking for action or trouble or sin. Women stand on street corners offering their bodies for sale.

HOOKER 1

I give the best BJs in AC.

HOOKER 2

She sure is ugly but she sure is good!

HOOKER 1

You can come on my face if you like.

SPENCER LUDWIG

No. Thank you.

SPENCER LUDWIG walks quickly on.

EXT. PACIFIC AVENUE—NIGHT

SPENCER LUDWIG looks in the window of the Junior Prada shop. His lips move as he scans the clothing on display. He is calculating whether he has enough money to buy everything on display. SPENCER LUDWIG walks on.

INT. HORSESHOE CASINO CARD ROOM

SPENCER LUDWIG sits at the poker table with a look of fierce concentration and a small pile of chips in front of him.

INT. HORSESHOE CASINO CARD ROOM

SPENCER LUDWIG, in exactly same position and with same expression as before, now has a large pile of chips in front of him.

INT. HORSESHOE CASINO CARD ROOM

SPENCER LUDWIG walks to the cashier's cage.

SPENCER LUDWIG
I'd like to register, for the tournament.

THE CASHIER puts out a hand. SPENCER is about to pass over all his chips. He stops. He squeezes his left wrist with his right hand.

EXT. HORSESHOE CASINO—DAY

SPENCER LUDWIG pushes past a HOTEL CLEANER who is mopping the driveway. SPENCER hails a cab, which swerves to the kerb.

INT. ATLANTIC GOLD PAWNBROKER—DAY

PAWNBROKER
It's to cover our costs.

SPENCER LUDWIG
What costs? You've only had the
watch a few hours.

PAWNBROKER
Terms and conditions, my friend.
I think I apprised you of the sliding scale.

SPENCER LUDWIG passes over a large bundle of banknotes. THE
PAWNBROKER waits. SPENCER gets out more money and flicks it
under the security glass.

EXT. ATLANTIC AVENUE—DAY

SPENCER LUDWIG walks fast, his left hand firmly in trouser pocket.
A glint of gold in the street lights.

INT. HORSESHOE CASINO

Spencer is exhausted. He leans, eyes closed, against the wall of
the elevator car. He strokes the face of his father's watch.

He had felt its absence as a bereavement, the absence of his
father's hand gripping his wrist.

Spencer returns to the room. The maid has been in and restored
the room to some shape of order. He opens the safe, puts in
his watch, locks the safe—and then unlocks it again, and clasps

the watch back to his wrist again, pinching the skin, squeezing hairs around the gold.

It is a relief to be alone. Spencer lies on the bed, flicks through television channels, switches the television off, glances at the room service menu, orders a BLT and a Heineken from a voice that sounds nothing like Dwight's, switches the television on again, the baffling pointlessness of *Hogan's Heroes*, and exhales a long, slow, rumbling breath, which feels like the first time he has properly exhaled since this road trip began.

He wants sex, he wants beer, he wants sleep, he wants food. He is looking forward to his BLT with a hunger that tastes like lust. He loosens his trousers, briefly considers masturbation, but settles instead for a most luxuriant stretch that seems to invite every muscle of his body.

Impatient for his order, he hears a sound in the corridor, hopes it is the waiter, but there is no one there, just a door closing at the far end of the corridor, a woman's laugh left behind. Returning to the room, he notices first that the backgammon set is not in its proper place on the table by the window, before he sees, rejected on the floor, perhaps kicked half beneath the bed by the foot of a careless or negligent maid, his father's surgical collar.

Seized by a fluttery panic that he blames his stepmother for—this must be how she feels when anything happens out of her control, an event that she has not sanctioned: the vase in the hallway is an inch away from its regular place, the bread basket in the restaurant does not contain the usual rolls, Jacksie's weekly telephone call is twenty minutes early, the President is caught out in a lie. He resents that he should feel this way too; but his father is not in the bathroom, or in the hall. His father is his responsibility, but Jimmy Ludwig has always been impatient of authority, so perhaps the surprise should be that he had settled, or appeared to, for so long under Spencer's benevolent rule.

Carrying the grimy surgical collar, Spencer leaves the hotel room. The elevator that takes him downstairs is irksomely slow. He wishes that Dwight were still here because Dwight, in a quietly authoritative manner that Spencer's stepmother ought to envy, seemed to be in control of most objects and events in his hotel. But Dwight is gone, Dwight is not in the lobby, and neither is Spencer's father.

He had left him bloodied and sleeping. Anything might have happened to him. He could have died in his sleep, and the supposed order of the room is the flustered result of the hospitality business hiding traces of death. He could be roaming the streets, tottering on the sidewalks, adrift and confused.

Spencer looks for his father in the places that they have been to together. But he is not one of the occupants of the electric wheelchairs in the all-you-can-eat death buffet. He is not on the casino floor at the blackjack table that has been especially widened for the needs of cripples and the dying. He is not sitting outside looking at the Boardwalk or the ocean or the desolate rickshaw riders, shivering in the unseasonal chill. Neither is he gazing in aficionado pleasure at the workings of the vertical blue fountain or sitting in the Sports Book or the crowded festival bar. Spencer goes to the Italian bar, to drink the beer he has missed in the room. He wonders how long he can avoid the possibilities. He might even have to call his step-mother.

And there his father is, in his wheelchair at the table where they had drunk with Drussilla and Tanya. In the absence of the collar, his chin is pressed tight to his chest as he rolls the dice and moves, with wavering hands, his backgammon pieces.

His opponent is a man of indeterminate age, probably closer to Jimmy Ludwig's age than Spencer's. He has very grey, papery skin that clings tight to the bones of his face in some places and sags in others. When he removes his baseball cap, deciding what to do with the six and two he has just rolled, he reveals a head that is entirely bald and Spencer wonders whether there is a similar absence of hair everywhere else on his body.

Spencer's father is dressed in his food-spattered chinos, the yellow polo shirt that must have cost him agonies to force over his head, grey windcheater that once was white. Apart from his uncombed hair, falling away from the scarlet wound on his scalp, he looks unharmed, at ease. Maybe he is imperishable.

'I've been looking for you,' Spencer says.

'I'm here,' his father says.

'This your son? Your dad is a heck of a player.'

'He has his moments.'

Jimmy Ludwig's opponent sits with the stoicism and still-ness of a professional gambler. Spencer's anxieties about his missing father are replaced by a fearfulness of the opponent he has chosen to play against or, more likely, who has chosen him, a senescent mark.

Other than a barman who pretends to clean glasses, Spencer's father and his backgammon partner had the place to them-selves before Spencer's arrival.

The opponent tries to escape one of his pieces from Jimmy Ludwig's home board. Spencer's father throws a four and a one, which allows him to hit the piece his opponent had left behind, but not to cover it.

'Nerves of steel,' the opponent says. He rolls a double six but the point is occupied and he may not escape the bar.

Spencer hates watching people play backgammon. He only learned the game out of a kind of bored desperation, sitting on his father's boat, watching his father and stepmother find another way of ignoring him. By the end of the summer, he recognised when his stepmother was making mistakes and, with only days to go before his return to London, he was brave enough to correct her. Magnanimously, she allowed him to take her place at the board, and his father, being a practical man as well as a ruthless one, soon declared his son to be the preferable opponent. Nonetheless, like the sensation of sitting in the back seat of a car, watching backgammon being played arouses in Spencer no sentimentality or calm, just a re-eruption of the resentments and stifled furies of his childhood.

'What are the stakes?'

'Two-five,' the opponent says.

It's a curious, perhaps local, way of saying twenty-five cents a point, but Spencer is anyway relieved that his father has not opened himself to a fleecing from a rounder. His father always plays for twenty-five cents, and has never changed his mind for anybody, so there is no reason that he will start now.

Jimmy Ludwig offers his opponent a double, which is politely rejected.

'Ah! No guts,' Jimmy Ludwig expostulates in disgust and watches his opponent write down the new score on the bar napkin.

'*Dad!*'

'He's quite a character, your dad. I'm sorry I can't play much longer.'

Is this the pre-emptive apology for the hit-and-run? Spencer wants to know who's winning. He can't see the numbers on the napkin, but, as he would like at least one Ludwig man to represent some kind of courtesy to the world, he just quietly lifts his father's fallen cane off the ground, hooks it over the basket of his wheelchair, and asks if anyone would like a drink.

No one would, except for him, and he sips his beer and leans back in his chair until his father snaps at him to sit straight, and blames him for the game that he subsequently loses.

Spencer sits sullenly after that, surreptitiously leaning back on the rear legs of his chair. The opponent, whose hairless smoothness is never ruffled by Jimmy Ludwig's speech-play, the *Disgusting!*s and *Incredible!*s and *You lucky dog!*s, does everything carefully, rolling his dice, moving his pieces, noting down the score. Spencer watches three boards, two of which the opponent wins.

'OK, I'm going to have to let you go,' he says.

'Well it's been nice, I thank you,' Jimmy Ludwig says, returned to courtesy again, and Spencer has never realised before quite how calculated are his father's moods at the table. His father reaches out a hand to shake his opponent's, apologises for having to go to use the men's room, and whizzes out of the bar on his electric chair.

'Looked like quite a game. My father is, you know . . .' Spencer says.

'Please don't mention it. He's a very engaging gentleman.'

'I'm not sure if gentleman is quite the word,' Spencer says, but seeing an expression of shock slip across the man's face at a son's lack of veneration for his elders, he erupts with a little chuckle as if he had been making a joke. A moment of awkward silence is broken by his father's opponent picking up the scoresheet.

'OK. I guess it's time we should settle our accounts. You can act for your father, I suppose?'

'What was the final score?'

'He was nineteen points up. It went to and fro, but that was the score at the end of the day.'

'That makes, what, four seventy-five?'

'That's what I make it too. My name is Bob, by the way.'

'How are you, Bob? I'm Spencer.'

'Pretty good, pretty good,' says Bob, reaching into a pocket of his slacks.

Spencer is comfortable in this sort of exchange and he rather likes the seriousness with which Bob is treating the transaction.

'So,' Spencer says, 'if I give you a quarter, then you can give me five.'

'Sure. That will make it easier.'

Apart from the moment of Spencer's disrespect for his elders, it has all been very amiable, but the mood is abruptly broken.

'What the hell is that?!' Bob wants to know, staring at the offering in Spencer's hand.

'A quarter. I thought we said . . .?'

'Yeah, yeah. Look, joker boy, it doesn't pay to make enemies with the likes of me, but here you go, take your fucking money. And I don't want to see you again, you understand me?'

There is something very chilling in Bob's face. The hairless man is hard to read, Spencer would not like to encounter him at the poker table, or indeed anywhere, and this does not seem like bluster or a bluff. He fumbles with the wad, replaces some bills with more from another, even larger wad and passes the bundle to Spencer.

'Look, I'm sorry, I don't know. I just . . .'

'But nothing. Fuck off.'

He suspects the man is insane, but he is gone now, leaving a door swinging behind him, leaving an untaken quarter in Spencer's right hand and an unlikely roll of bills in his left.

Spencer catches up with his father outside on the Boardwalk. His father is sometimes motivated, at times of triumph or stress, to gaze upon the sea.

'Uh. Do you know how much you were playing for?'

'What?'

'That game. That backgammon game you were just playing.'

'The guy was called Bob.'

'Yes. I know. He introduced himself.'

'A very pleasant fellow.'

'Well. Be that as it may. What were the stakes?'

'What?'

'How much were you playing for? How much a point?'

'The usual. Why? Didn't he pay?'

'He paid. You thought you were playing for twenty-five cents a point?'

'Something wrong?'

'Nothing wrong. Oh here. By the way. Here's your collar. You should be wearing it.'

'By the way, so where's my money?'

They are on the ramp that leads from the Boardwalk to the sea. The morning sun is rising, the wind is blowing, and the wad of Spencer's father's money is making a priapic bulge in Spencer's right trouser pocket.

'Your . . .?'

'You heard.'

Spencer's father's hair rises and falls in the breeze. Spencer pats and finger-combs it back into place, smoothing the strands over the eggshell scalp, bare except for the wounds that Spencer had inflicted in the night; and Spencer's father tilts his head, relaxing into the contact. Ignobly, Spencer feels as if he has won a victory here, although he is not sure who is his defeated opponent.

Spencer lifts the bankroll out of his pocket. He holds it up to the breeze, and it would be so easy now just to let it go, to watch the notes tumbling and swooping in the breeze. If this were a film then that is what he would probably do, the final image, banknotes flying like hungry birds over the Atlantic City beach, to some people's consternation and others' glee.

So he lets two go, just to test their flight, and to see how hard it would be to film. If real money were to be used—and wouldn't that be a grand thing?—then he would have only one shot at it. He lets the notes go, one catches the wind and it does just what he had hoped it would, fluttering, swooping, a wild rising, invisible for a moment in front of a cloud, and then falling, a sudden dip, holding for a moment about ten feet from the sand. It startles a solitary beachcomber, who makes an instinctive grab for it even though it is impossible, out of reach, and his hand grasps at air as the note rises again, and drifts over the ocean. The other bill falls beneath the notice of the wind and drops beside Jimmy Ludwig's wheelchair.

Spencer's father reaches for it. Spencer wonders if he might use Monopoly money, whether it could have the same effect, green and purple and brown play notes drifting over Atlantic Avenue and Pacific Avenue and the Boardwalk and the beach and the ocean.

His father can't quite pick up the hundred-dollar bill. His fingertips scrabble against the paper, which rests primly against the wooden ramp. Spencer reaches down to retrieve it for him.

'What's this?'

'Your money.'

'Too much.'

'Or not enough.'

'What?'

'There was a . . . misunderstanding. You weren't playing for the stakes you thought you were.'

'I don't want it. Give me the five dollars.'

'You thought you were playing for twenty-five cents a point. Actually you were playing for two hundred and fifty dollars a point. You understand? Just as well you won. We'd've been in some kind of trouble if you'd lost. That guy you were playing against? I'm not sure I took to him.'

'I don't understand you.'

Is it possible to steal money from someone who doesn't know he has it? Of course it is, that's what makes bankers rich. Spencer has his entry to the tournament, but he tries again to explain to his father, backgammon stakes, twenty-five cents, two hundred and fifty dollars, misunderstandings, Bob, but his father stubbornly clings to his demand for the four dollars and seventy-five cents that he thinks he is owed; and the sun is going up, and the beach is getting warmer, and his father is becoming irritated by his own incomprehension of what Spencer is trying to explain, and by being thwarted of his winnings, the trophy of his accomplishment, the proof that he can still compete with, and triumph over, other men.

'I need to get some sleep,' Spencer says.

'Aren't you going gambling?' his father says.

'Oh. Yes. Sure. The poker tournament. But that's later, in the afternoon. Do you mind?'

Spencer helps his father manoeuvre back towards the Boardwalk.

'I don't mind. But I want my five dollars.'

'Here. I think I have it.' Spencer roots through his trousers, manages to find a crumpled five-dollar bill. He smooths Lincoln's face before passing it to his father.

'Come on. I'm going to get some sleep. I'll buy you breakfast on the way.'

'What time is it?'

Spencer rolls up his sleeve to show his father his watch.

'How are you enjoying it?'

'I love it,' Spencer says, and he thinks he does.

Chapter Ten

The winner of the Second Annual Atlantic City Poker Classic will receive $50,000. Spencer has bought his ticket, received his seat allocation, and performed his pre-tournament preparations. He has emptied bowels and bladder, bathed, bought his bag of mixed nuts, his bottle of water. Dwight, before his disappearance, had supplied several hours of boxing DVDs that will keep his father in one, predictable place. Jimmy Ludwig, his cut still seeping beneath the Band-Aid on his head, a bruise growing around it, purple and black and red, has sandwiches and water on the table beside his armchair, his favourite boxer, Thomas 'The Hit Man' Hearns, on the television screen in front of him; and Spencer steps reluctant and thrilled into that zone familiar to con-men and utopianists where he has already, in his mind, won the tournament and the money.

It is a glorious masochistic exalted feeling, to walk down a boulevard of shops and believe that anything in them could be his. This must be how his daughter thinks. This must be what his father wanted from America.

He will repay his father for his inadvertent loan with one hundred per cent interest or, better, bestow a gift to charity in his father's name—plant a tree in Warsaw, make an endowment for students from war zones to study engineering and law. He will sell back the wheelchair and top up the proceeds with some more cash for the Baumbachs. He could buy this for his daughter, and this for her mother, and this for his father, and this for Abbie, and this for Michelle, and this (*Fuck you!*) for Rick Violet, and these things for himself, a dandy, a superman, Gentleman Spencer Ludwig, ivory toothpick, gold-topped cane, diamond tooth, *I raise, I reraise!*, a tip of his hat.

Excuse me, gentlemen, they're waiting for me on set. To imagine it is to own it.

Perhaps Spencer's historical loftiness is the outsider's ease. If you can't buy, then you're not implicated. Splash him into the mainstream and he might swim no more gracefully than any of them.

But he doesn't have the money, to imagine it is to curse it into non-being, he hasn't won the poker tournament, it hasn't even started yet.

He walks along Pacific Avenue. A seagull with a broken wing flaps futilely in the road. Sedans and taxicabs swerve to avoid it.

Spencer, who has never believed in omens before, braves the traffic. He stands between lanes, one foot on a broken line, the other beside, almost touching, the damaged bird. Cars swerve around them both now as Spencer softens his outraged sense of squeamishness, forces his unwilling hands to pick up the bird, which flaps even harder now. He had not realised quite how wide a seagull's wingspan is. He averts his face, he clenches the frantic wing tight, imagining himself to be Officer Porrelli and the seagull a lame malefactor. The seagull's heart beats against his chest as Spencer scurries to the safety of the sidewalk. And what now? Is there a hospital ward for damaged birds? The

Peter Lawford wing, maybe. Spencer stands with a maimed seagull in his arms. He rests it down on the sidewalk and walks to the lights of the casino.

Spencer starts the tournament steadily. In the first rounds, he comes to an understanding of the players at his table, who he needs to make a stand against, whose chips are there for the taking. The player to his right conforms to a particularly detestable species of poker sub-chic, with his peculiarly shaped, lumpy body, the sunglasses, DiamondPoker T-shirt, iPod, cap from the Bellagio casino, and the undeserved self-regard of a boy whose mother made the mistake of loving him too much.

Spencer's rhythm and timing are good. He is able to push people off pots and when he does go to a showdown, his is always the winning hand. The world shrinks to the felt. At spare moments he chats to the player two to his left, a young Brazilian, who plays with aggressive verve and charm, and has a taste, which Spencer shares, for psychedelic music of the 1960s.

The Brazilian boy breaks off a conversation about Skip Spence to retreat into himself as he gets involved in a large pot against the lumpy boy. The Brazilian pushes the remainder of his chips in front of him and leans back. His opponent flicks the edges of his cards, counts out the amount it will cost him to call, and stares at the Brazilian through the mirror of his shades. He dwells some more. Reluctantly, eventually, he folds. The Brazilian boy grins and shows his cards, a seven and a two, garbage, a bluff, and he rakes in the pot with a delightfully innocent glee.

The Brazilian can't stop grinning. 'I love poker, I love it!' he says. 'The emotion! All the different things you feel, the heart goes bump-bump-bump!'

Spencer loves it too, especially now, when he's in the form and concentration of his life. He needs a red ace, he gets it. He calls a bet on the turn because he knows he can bully his opponent out of the pot with a bet on the river. He has more chips than anyone else at his table, he is an early leader of the tournament.

'Os Mutantes,' the Brazilian boy says. 'You're in the zone,' and Spencer half nods in acknowledgement.

He is in the zone. Nothing else exists. Until it does; he is moved, to balance a short-handed table on the far side of the room. He carries his chips in a plastic rack and his jacket on his arm and his bag of nuts clenched in his mouth, and he follows the tournament director to his new seat, where the back of his head is exposed to an aisle, the air is colder, and he is wedged uncomfortably tight between two large men, who are, like the rest of the table, hostile strangers. He thinks of lumpy boy with a surprising sentimentality. He wants to be back at his first table, where everything was known and under his control; he makes an early-position raise with ace-queen, misses the flop, and gets involved in a skirmish with one of the large men on the big blind, who bullies him out of the pot on the turn and then shows his inferior ace. He calls a raise, and then cravenly folds when the raiser makes a continuation bet on the flop. His concentration has slipped and his chips are dribbling away and he becomes over-aware of unnecessary things, the disconcerting angle of the dealer's name badge, the bitter, not entirely unpleasant odour of his neighbours who are squeezing against him, and the whir of the air conditioning, which reminds him of his father's oxygen machine.

Spencer wins a few chips back, loses more, and as players are eliminated around him, and tables broken up, he is moved again twice. He is sitting again now with both lumpy boy and the Brazilian. The dinner break approaches, Spencer's stack is small and hunted. He goes all-in three times in a row, hoping to double up or end what is becoming a torment. His place is not here. He had been foolish to believe it might be. He is called the third time, by a player with even fewer chips than he has, whose pair of kings holds up rather easily against Spencer's 6–3 off-suit. Trying to avoid the Brazilian boy's eyes, in case he sees reproach in them, he inadvertently catches the gaze of an old grinder who reminds him of Gambler Bob, and whose expression offers him the coldest kind of pity.

During the break Spencer takes a walk along the seafront. He should check on his father but he doesn't want to inflict his sense of failure on anyone else, or maybe just doesn't want his father, with his expert sense for other people's weakness, to sniff it.

Going along the Boardwalk, Spencer imagines it populated with characters from his own films. That could be Gold the architect solemnly taking out one of his biros to draw a line in the air in congruence with the square roof of the Wild West casino, and he sees Robert W, reborn as a beachcomber, kicking through the sand, his hat pulled down low against the sun. He sees the figures but can't picture the faces, he can recall John Wayne's face, or Dominique Sanda's, or Martin LaSalle's better than any of his own. But what he can perfectly imagine is his daughter, her coiled body, ready to lift into flight, her narrow features, her hair falling down in a new, favoured way.

Spencer Ludwig walks back to the casino, he is about to be knocked out of a tournament, he has reached no resolution with his father, the Atlantic breeze cuts through. Taxi-rickshaw riders huddle inside their vehicles. Outside the Horseshoe two attenuated shabby men stare through the glass doors. Spencer joins them. Their lack of money forbids entry. This is democracy and they are disqualified from participating in it. Lights and colour are forbidden them.

He goes down to the underground car park, where his father's car sits, peaceable and scarred. Spencer gets behind the driving wheel. He has done this before, in other cars of his father's, similarly black and leathered, child Spencer at the wheel imagining all encumbrances gone while driving fast to elsewhere. The air is somewhat rank in this car. On the back seat a sealed plastic bag contains a rotting banana and two slightly gooey plums.

He could stay here, build his life in this car. The back seat is roomy enough to sleep on, or the front passenger seat, which fully reclines, might be even better; the back seat could be his daytime space, that's where he'd do his entertaining and play internet poker. He could breakfast and dine on room service, he wouldn't even have to leave the garage for drive-through meals.

It would be good to build a life in this car, a better prospect than returning to the tournament just to die there. But this is reborn Spencer now, the man becoming something new. No obstacle too high, no humiliation too gross.

The tournament area has shrunk. There are only four tables left. Spencer tries to remember where he was sitting.

'Hey Anglo! You're over here.' The call is from the Brazilian boy sitting at his table.

'I thought I'd maybe just watch.'

'Chip and a chair, man.'

Indeed. At a seat untenanted apart from Spencer's jacket hanging loosely off its back, a bag of assorted nuts dwarfs his tiny stack of chips. Spencer sits down, just in time for his hand not to be declared dead. His heart is dully knocking. He tells himself that he won't look at his cards, he'll just have to go all-in regardless of his holding. The peculiarly shaped young man, whose mother loved him too much, is performing masturbatory riffling manoeuvres with his towers of chips. Spencer can hold his chips easily in the palm of one hand.

The cards are shuffled and dealt. Spencer is in the big blind, lumpy mother-love, on his immediate left, is under the gun.

'Sir. Sir?' says the lumpy boy. 'Can I see how many chips you have?'

Spencer, not bothering to hide his disconsolation, opens his hand, letting his chips roll to the felt. He is pleased, in a doleful sort of way, that they roll in together and turn over together.

'All-in blind. Raise of a thousand,' says the dealer.

That wasn't what he was intending, but it doesn't matter. The Brazilian boy calls, so does lumpy boy, so does the old grinder, whose skin is slightly greyer than his hair. Spencer makes his preparations to leave. He puts on his jacket, brushes the dust left by his nuts into the cup of his hand and sprinkles it beneath his chair. He doesn't look at his cards or follow the action, there doesn't seem to be any point. His attention turns back to the table when he sees the dealer push a pile of chips his way.

'Nice catch,' lumpy boy says.

'Thank you,' says Spencer, with slightly greater sincerity.

The heartfelt magic of the Coup Classique. His stack is still small but at least he is alive. He has five times the big blind. He could even afford to pass the next hand.

Spencer raises the next hand. Five players call him, including lumpy boy. This is not good, to be out of position against multiple opponents, including the most aggressive player at the table. He looks at his cards to see five of spades, two of clubs, one of the worst starting hands in poker, and not the exit hand he would have chosen. The flop comes down 349, rainbow. Spencer checks. Lumpy boy makes a small bet, everyone else passes. Spencer calls with the open-ended straight draw.

The turn is a king. Spencer checks, and he hopes this might be taken for aggression, not weakness, the nemesis setting out to trap, maybe Spencer can see the river card without putting in the rest of his chips. Lumpy boy bets, putting Spencer all-in.

'I have to call,' Spencer says, tossing in the last of his chips.

'On their backs please, gentlemen,' the dealer says.

They table their cards. Spencer shows his lunge at the straight. Lumpy boy turns over pocket aces.

'It's OK, you have outs,' the Brazilian boy says.

'Only four of 'em,' says the grey old gambler. 'I folded a pair of sixes.'

'Make that three. I folded an ace,' says a player at the far end of the table.

Spencer instantly hates both men, more than he can ever remember hating anyone before. Life in the car would be so much better than this. He would even rather still be outside in the cold, standing peering in at the lights.

'Good luck,' the Brazilian boy says.

'Thank you,' Spencer says.

It saddens Spencer even further that he will never know the Brazilian boy's name.

The dealer turns over the river card, which is the ace of diamonds, giving lumpy boy a set of aces but making Spencer's straight.

Almost apologetically, Spencer rakes in the chips.

'Nice catch,' the lumpy boy says again, burning at him.

'Thank you,' Spencer says.

'Slow-playing rockets,' the old gambler says, shaking his head in disapproval.

Lumpy boy's sunglasses tip down his nose. He rubs his face, which is blushing—his father has caught him out in a lie, the mirror tells the truth, his mother might no longer love him.

Hatred and fear and self-pity bite into the air around him. Spencer likes to have enemies at the table. It gives him focus.

Now he has the chips, now he has to play, and play Spencer does. He plays far more pots than his cards could possibly allow. He catches the Brazilian boy out in one of his moments of bluffing flair. He in turn bluffs lumpy boy out of a sizeable pot. And then he comes up against the old grinder.

They are down to the last thirteen players. All of them are in the money. Nine will return for tomorrow's final table, where the big prizes will be won. Soon the tournament director will come by with plastic bags to store the survivors' chips for the night. The rail birds will drift away. Spencer's bag of nuts is almost empty. He picks through the dust, searching for an almond among the rejected cashews, and raises on the button with ace-queen of clubs.

The future is everywhere, even in Atlantic City. The grinder, who could be Spencer in twenty years' time, every situation seen before, every action performed with slow deliberation, considers his response.

'I've never been to Brazil,' Spencer tells the Brazilian boy.

'Oh you should, man. It's beautiful. The girls are hot.'

'Or Argentina. I've always wanted to go to Argentina.'

'Yeah. Well. Argentina,' the Brazilian boy says.

'I'm going to travel,' Spencer says. 'I'm going to go places. And I'm going to make sure I take notice of everything I see. And I'm going to get healthy, sort out my diet, get into regular exercise. And I'm going to be a better father, and *kind*. I'm going to be a kinder man.'

'Hey, Self-Improvement Guy,' the dealer says. 'The action is on you.'

The grinder has reraised. Spencer does not like this. A little meekly, Spencer calls.

The flop comes down with the ten and six of clubs, and the queen of hearts. Spencer has top pair, and if another club falls he has the nut flush. The grinder bets, Spencer calls. The real action can come later. The turn is the king of clubs. The old grinder checks, Spencer bets his flush and the grinder calls. The river is the six of diamonds. The grinder checks. Spencer makes a small value bet, and the grinder check-raises all-in.

He wants to call, but more importantly, the old grinder wants him to call. Spencer can feel it, the ache of desire in the grinder's implacable stillness.

Sometimes, Spencer would throw his chances to the winds, the vertigo of surrender. It is easier, more nourishing, to throw yourself into the abyss than to be a bystander at its edge. But Spencer makes himself take a little longer over the action than he would choose to. He looks again at the old grinder.

'I pass,' Spencer says, throwing his cards into the muck.

The grinder is surprised, cheated of his consummation.

'Good fold, son,' he says, graciously showing his pocket tens for a full house and gathering in the chips that are so much fewer than they should be.

And Spencer, surgeon, duellist, artist, is back to raising and bluff-reraising and dodging and twisting and using his chips as a blade and a scalpel and a brush.

The Brazilian is getting short-stacked. He goes all-in. Spencer calls with ten-eight of spades. Lumpy boy calls as well. No one bets on the flop, which is ace, ace, ten, all different suits, rainbow. Lumpy boy bets the turn, which is a six. Spencer doesn't trust lumpy boy, who is a better player than Spencer would like him to be. Spencer calls. The river is a two. Spencer checks. Lumpy boy announces he's going all-in. Spencer will have a few chips left over if he calls, but hardly any, and there is little reason to risk his tournament life now.

'He's got bubkus.' It is his father's voice, low and resonant.

'That's Yiddish for nothing,' Spencer says, and looks hopefully up from the table, the hands of his opponents, the veins upon them, muscles flexing as they fiddle with their chips, the dealer's stillness, and lumpy boy's eyes as he removes his sunglasses to reveal something milder than Spencer had expected, close to Jacksie's look of perpetual hurt, the rail birds watching the tournament, and Spencer is hoping for a flash of a canary-yellow polo shirt, his father's smile, the whir of an electric wheelchair. But Spencer's father is not there. No one has heard what he has heard, and Spencer's translation is taken for British eccentricity, or the angle-shooter's unorthodox attempt to gain some response and information from lumpy boy.

'I call,' Spencer says.

It was a bluff. His father's voice was right. Spencer wins the pot, knocking out the Brazilian as well as lumpy boy, who doesn't even bother to show his cards as he gets up from the table and reaches for a beer from a similarly shaped friend. The other table has lost a player as well. One more elimination and play will be over for the day. The next hand—but there is no next hand. The world intervenes, announcing itself in the bulky shape of Jenny De Soto. She is trying to make her way to the tournament area, but a floor man is blocking her way.

Spencer Ludwig learned to lip-read watching silent movies. At an early age he recognised that the lines the actors were speaking seldom bore any relation to the words posted up on the inter-titles: *I want a hamburger . . . What are you doing later?* Even the infamous moment, in a Mack Sennett comedy, *Who's got the cocaine?* And the floor man is saying, *You got to check your bags, ma'am.* And Jenny De Soto, her face bobbing up over the shoulder of the floor man, has finally found where Spencer is sitting and she is saying to him, repeating the same two words,

Your father. Your father. Your father.

Decisions, not results is the old poker maxim. That is what you are judged by, maybe even in his father's court. Spencer leaves his chips where they fall and his bag of nuts behind.

His father lies in a hospital bed, rigged up to drip bags and oxygen tank, eyes closed, the bed cover pulled poignantly up to just below his chin as if this is a child lying here, who needs protection both from inside and out, the viruses that threaten his fragile body, the shadow creatures who haunt his imagination at night. An arm flutters from beneath the covers to wipe something away from his nose, and there is hardly any flesh on the arm, even the area between thumb and forefinger is wasted away, a deep hollow between bones.

'Dad,' Spencer says.

He is ready to mourn. His stepmother was right, this has all been madcap murderous, he had no business removing his father from a world of medical appointments and jigsaws and silence, Jimmy's constitution is not strong enough to bear any disruption to his routine.

'Get me some,' his father says with his eyes still closed as if he might be dreaming.

A father's job is to provide and protect. Jimmy Ludwig always prided himself on being a good provider. But how could he be an adequate protector if he was the one who caused most alarm?

'It's OK. You don't need to talk.'

Perhaps Spencer's voice soothes him. His father falls silent again.

Spencer calls Mary, hospital telephone to mobile. The bill for this is unthinkable but he needs to speak to her.

'Hey.'

'Hi Daddy.'

He doesn't have anything to say to her, even though he longs to prove that he can protect her, as he sits watching his sleeping, drugged, betubed father, he just wants to hear her voice. He asks her questions about Poppy and Lily and Rose and Jasmine, and falls in love again with the timbre of his daughter's voice.

He realises that he is looking for a benediction from his father. What his father has taught him: how to fold a towel and a T-shirt, how to roll up a hosepipe and a rope. His father has given him a gold watch, a sense of history, and a partial, distempered view of his first marriage. He wants more. His father once advised him, *Don't shit where you eat*, and tried to impress upon him the importance of a good credit rating. Spencer never quite understood the first advice, failed to follow the second, and he wants more fatherly wisdom than that.

'Don't promise more than you can deliver,' he says to his daughter, interrupting a description of some inexplicable school event that seems to involve a piano, a football and someone called Dijon. And, when there is no reply, he adds, 'Inspiration is what happens when you don't know what you're doing but you're doing the best you can.'

He should be able to come up with more, but he has time, he supposes he does. Here they're reaching the end. If his father should wake again, and speak more cogently, it might be their last conversation, or the next to last. Doesn't that mean it should have more weight to it? Aren't there things you've longed to say? Sins you've wanted to confess? But Jimmy Ludwig is not a Christian, he does not believe in redemption, he hardly believes in love.

'What's that?'

'Are you playing poker?'

'Well, no. Yes. Sort of.'

'Are you winning?'

'I was, but . . . hold on, I better go. Papa Jimmy is stirring.'

Spencer's father is sitting up in bed. He's swinging his legs to the floor. He stands, totters, sits down again, his robe open at the back, almost hairless legs, a flat pale arse, gaunt except for the waves of flesh above either hip.

'Need a leak,' he says.

'You don't have to, it's all taken care of.'

'Disgusting,' his father says, looking sourly at the tubes leading out of his body into the bags, yellow, red, brown and gold, the colours of the flag of a failing principality.

With a heave and a push and a grab at the trolley, Spencer's father, defying gravity and weakness, has hoiked himself to his feet.

Jimmy Ludwig takes a step, forces his chin and eyes up as high as they will go, plans his route ahead.

'It's not necessary. It's all done with drips and catheters,' Spencer says.

He watches, in a kind of awe, his father roll the trolley along the floor, steering and leaning on it to reach the bathroom. Spencer follows, ready to catch him if he should fall, unable to intervene. Jimmy Ludwig stands at the toilet bowl, legs slightly turned in at the knees. He fumbles at his crotch, and notices something for the first time, the catheter that is installed into his penis, says *Huh*, in a surprised way, as he commences nonetheless to piss, the urine spraying around. Somehow— skilful fingers (he was an engineer before he was an attorney), the absolute will to urinate on his own terms—he manages to disengage the plastic tap and tubing that had been fixed into his urethra. His urine flows in a straight line now and he leans against the bathroom wall, as if posing in his triumph.

A nurse helps Spencer return his father to the bed. She reinstalls the catheter.

'What a naughty boy,' she says. 'You know I've never seen anyone do that before. Your father is a remarkable man.'

And a sick one. He had been rescued in the hotel lobby, looking for his son, lurching from palm tree to front desk, waving his arms in the air, unable to breathe.

'And how is he now?'

'He's stable. Let him rest a while. You can take him home tomorrow.'

Where is this home that she talks of so lightly? It could be their hotel room, which, in a will-to-sordidness, is daily resisting the efforts of the maid to clean it. (Spencer has had two conversations with the maid, whose name is, she seemed to claim, Cuba. Spencer had asked her if she would consent to be filmed, because if Spencer could borrow a camera he would like a session with her for his project, *The Invisibles*, whose only criterion for subjects' inclusion is that they must live some kind of public life that most people ignore. Their second conversation consisted largely of him apologising for the misunderstandings he had caused in the first.)

Maybe home could be found elsewhere in Atlantic City, with

Jenny De Soto and the mother she probably lives with, a world of film references and, he suspects, cats, or in some modern mansion that belongs to a nervous man who owes a favour to Gambler Bob, or further along the road, a future mark on an unread map, a dot on the horizon that grows towards their fast-moving car.

Or, the sensible thing, return his father to Manhattan and Museum Tower, jigsaw puzzles and decline. And Spencer will go off again, accommodated to his discontents, otherwise this has been nothing significant, just a detour.

Or this is it, Jenny De Soto's option three becoming manifest, they've tasted too much, put themselves out of reach, the nurse was appeasing the moment with her airy talk of home, and wherever that could have been, it's long ago—and maybe Jimmy Ludwig never had one—and there is only one way to end their movie, 'the usual one', but Spencer does not want it to be here, a hospital bed in the Frank Sinatra Wing.

And what is Spencer without his father to look after, to fight? He might be set free, but to do what?

His father makes efforts to talk, to make himself understood, beneath the drugs, through the tubes. He weeps in his frustration. His arm falls exhausted to the bed.

'Try again,' says merciless Spencer.

'This is like . . .' his father says.

'Like?'

'The man's hands.'

'Who?'

'Going away. The man's hands.'

'What?'

'Your play.'

'Film?'

'The hand. The man's hands.'

'Whose hands?'

Then he sees it, perhaps as his father does, the final image of *Robert W's Last Walk*. And he wonders if this is what he became a film-maker for, to create an image that would burn in his father's imagination.

'And.'

'And what?' Spencer says.

But his father is sinking beneath the weight of his medication. He mutters words that Spencer cannot decipher. His eyes flutter closed again, and open, coquettishly, blink, and shut.

'No animals were harmed during the making of this picture,' Spencer says.

He has always wanted that as a tagline to one of his films, and he resolves that his next will have it, whether or not there are any animals involved. Spencer has always had trouble with his endings. Maybe the reason he likes *Robert W* so much is that the film and its ending justify each other more aptly than anything else he has made.

Red River ends with John Wayne and Montgomery Clift fighting, Walter Brennan grinning in the watching crowd, delighted that the (adopted) son is finally giving the 'father' the beating he needs—until it's broken up by a gunshot, Montgomery Clift's girl (and we know that in Westerns young women are the embodiments of virtue and the repositories of, among other things, truth) standing with a shotgun. 'Stop it! Stop it. Stop making a holy . . . [she fires another shot]. Stop it, I said. I'm mad. I'm good and mad and who wouldn't be!' And it goes on, her speech, outraged woman righteousness. When finally her energies are spent and she quits the scene, Wayne and Clift, abashed, sitting bruised in the dirt, look at each other. 'You better marry that girl, Matt,' Wayne says. Their dispute is over, the father finally recognises the son as his equal, and he draws the new brand for their ranch in the dust, both their initials together, like lovers' carved into a tree. 'You don't mind that, do you?' 'No.' And both smile, then look away, feeling an equivalent truth, an equal love. John Wayne looks at the brand he's drawn. 'You've earned it,' he says.

The movies might promise it, but it can't happen here.

In A Year of 13 Moons ends with the dead transsexual's family, neighbours, friends, nemeses, wandering disconsolately, standing, in the hall, rooms, stairway, of the apartment house, Elvira's voice speaking over it, the camera tracking around the interiors, past her body, and finishing, motionless now, it has nowhere else to go, with a shot of the empty staircase and Elvira's voice superseded by Connie Francis singing 'Schöner fremder Mann', the German version of 'Handsome Stranger' ('Handsome stranger, the time will come one day/When all my dreams become reality . . .'), until that gets stuck too, perpetually playing on a scratched groove.

The Big Heat, Glenn Ford telling the dying moll Gloria Grahame his sentimental domestic memories of his murdered wife. His face intent, his hair neatly greased, he doesn't even realise that Grahame has just died, her head turned to one side, so the ruined half of her face is hidden against her fur coat. But that's not the ending. He's back at his desk, reinstated, the awfulness is over, a helpful subordinate passes him a sharpened pencil, he sits down, 'How about some coffee, Hugo?' 'Coming right up, Sarge.' The telephone rings. 'Homicide? Bannion.' He picks up the pencil to make notes. It's a new case. A hit-and-run over on South Street. He takes his hat off the coatstand, walks out of the office. 'Keep the coffee hot, Hugo.' 'OK, sir.' The world keeps turning.

Which is why Spencer prefers Fassbinder to Lang, *13 Moons* to *Big Heat*. Some things should change the world, or finish it, its characters, the audience.

The Passenger might be closer to this road movie, even if Jack Nicholson was the driver, and now he's dead, leaving Maria Schneider alone, adrift, in southern Spain, seen through the bars of an old railing, waiting for the police car to arrive, and here it is, a bustle of policemen surrounds the wife of the character whose identity Nicholson had taken up; the camera watches them go into the hotel and we're outside on the street, looking at Nicholson's body on his hotel-room bed, again seen through bars, those of his window. 'Mrs Robinson,' a policeman says, 'do you recognise him?' The woman in a white trouser suit approaches the bed, briefly crouches beside the body, 'I never knew him,' she says; and the policeman turns to Maria Schneider, 'Do you recognise him?' 'Yes,' said so simply, and the next shot, a taxi drives away, leaving a twilit Andulasian village street, the mountains in the distance, the Hotel de La Gloria in the foreground, an old man walks his dog, another man stands in front of the hotel, a woman comes out to argue with him, as guitar music plays. She goes inside, he shouts derisorily after her, lights a cigarette and walks away. She comes back out, to sit on the step and do her knitting.

Spencer makes films so he will make another one. This is what he does.

The window in Jimmy Ludwig's intensive care room has no bars and neither does it offer a view of mountains. Spencer can see the backs of several Boardwalk casinos, their unbusiness ends, heavy unadorned blocks of concrete and brick, naked of lights or murals or promises.

The incantation of money. Spencer looks at last at Michelle's messages. It takes him a while to grasp that a cereal company is intent on paying him large amounts of money for stealing something from him that he didn't know he had: intellectual property, a television commercial; *One Door Opens*, and so does a corporation's very large wallet. The offers get larger with each message. They accuse Michelle and Spencer of playing hardball, which is not a game that Spencer thinks he knows the rules of. He goes to the window, tugs and pushes at the latch, and the more force he exerts, the more likely it seems that the latch is going to come away in his hands.

Alerted by the noise he is making, the nurse rushes back into the room.

'What are you doing? They don't open,' she says.

'Just wanted some air,' Spencer says, blushing under her scorn, thwarted in his aim of throwing out all Michelle's messages and watching them float or fall. Instead, he might have to humble himself to accept what he is offered.

'Your father'll be out a few hours,' the nurse says. 'We've given him a kiddie-dose of morphine, just so he can relax and breathe. You might want to take a break yourself.'

'Sure. Yes. Thank you.'

But the nurse spoke prematurely. Jimmy Ludwig's will has always been stronger than anything the world could throw at him. His eyes open again, he examines his son, he pulls out the words he wanted.

'Get a toaster-oven,' he says.

'I'll get a toaster-oven,' Spencer says.

'I thank you. You're a good man.'

That's a start. He waits for more.

'Stay away,' his father says.

'Oh.'

He interprets this as his father's aphasic attempt to say *Stay well*, but all the same it is not what he wants to hear.

'Good luck,' his father says. 'It's been nice.'

And his eyes close again as he curls towards sleep.

The author would like to thank the copyright holders of the following films for permission to reproduce images and lines:

Wise Blood, directed by John Huston © 1979 Janus Films
Atlantic City, directed by Louis Malle © 1980 Paramount
La Jetée, directed by Chris Marker © 1963 Argos Films
Red River, directed by Howard Hawks © 1948 MGM
The Conformist, directed by Norman Jewison © 1965 Warner Bros
The Big Heat, directed by Fritz Lang, script by Sydney Boehm © 1953 MGM
The Passenger, directed by Michelangelo Antonioni, script by Mark Peploe © 1975, courtesy of Jack Nicholson

Thanks are also due to Michael Vachon, Mathew Gibson, Kate Boxer, Glenn Haybittle, my family, and my father.